The Dance of the Ghost
and Other Stories

The Dance of the Ghost
and Other Stories

Surendra Mohanty

Translated from Odia by
Sambit Panigrahi

BLACK EAGLE BOOKS
2020

 BLACK EAGLE BOOKS

USA address:
7464 Wisdom Lane
Dublin, OH 43016

India address:
E/312, Trident Galaxy, Kalinga Nagar,
Bhubaneswar-751003, Odisha, India

E-mail: info@blackeaglebooks.org
Website: www.blackeaglebooks.org

First International Edition Published by
BLACK EAGLE BOOKS, 2020

The Dance of the Ghost and Other Stories
by **Surendra Mohanty**
Translated by **Sambit Panigrahi**

Cover & Interior Design: Ezy's Publication

ISBN- 978-1-64560-111-1 (Paperback)
Library of Congress Control Number: 2020945670

Printed in United States of America

Translator's Note

Surendra Mohanty, an eminent Odia writer and politician, was born on 21 June 1922 and died on 21 December 1990. A writer of unique creative acumen, Mohanty wrote many fictional and non-fictional works that continue to remain his significant contribution to the immense literary reservoir of Odia language. Apart from being a writer of great eminence and phenomenal reputability, Mohanty also held many important literary and political positions in the state and has contributed significantly to whatever sphere of activity he has been associated with. He was the president of Odisha Sahitya Academy from 1981 to 1987 and was also the first editor, and later chief editor for the newspaper *The Sambad*. He was a writer of short stories, novels, travelogues, criticism and biographies; he wrote around 50 books belonging to different genres. Some of his well-known novels are *Nilasaila* (*The Blue Mountain*) and *Andha Diganta* (*The Dark Horizon*) whereas some of his famous short stories include stories like *Mahanirvana* (*The Salvation*), *Yadubansa* (The Yadu Dynasty), *Mahanagarira Ratri* (*Night in the Metropolis*), *Rajadhani* (The Capital City), *Krushnachuda* (The Gulmohar) and *Ruti O Chandra* (Bread and The Moon).

Apart from being a litterateur of eminence, Mohanty was also a member of parliament many times from 1957 onwards.

Translating Surendra Mohanty is an experience in itself. It's widely acknowledged by literary critics across generations that Surendra Mohanty is perhaps at his creative best when he writes his short stories. The most interesting and attractive features of his stories are that they are not confined to any particular theme or area; rather, they range across a wide variety of subject matters including history, mythology, his contemporary society, the human individual etc. The wide spectrum of themes, areas and concerns that he encompasses in his stories attribute him wide acceptability and enormous respectability, amongst the audience, as a writer of eminence. Mohanty seems to have developed a particular interest in Buddhism and its history for which he has penned some of his stories like "Pita Putra" ("Father and Son") and "Mahanirvana" ("The Salvation") and in my estimation, some of Mohanty's finest stories are in fact his stories based on Buddhism and its history.

As mentioned by me, Mohanty also takes interest in mythology whose biggest testimony is his story "Srikrushnanka Sesha Hasa" (Srikrishna's Last Laugh) where he draws on certain important, interesting and not oft-mentioned episode of *The Mahabharata* and presents it before the audience in the form of a short story. By writing such stories, Mohanty not only displays another specimen of his phenomenal artistry as a creative writer, but also acquaints the readers with such forgotten or less known but important episodes of the great Indian epics like *The Mahabharata*.

But apart from mythological stories, Mohanty also focuses on realistic stories which have emerged from his own real-life experiences that range across different eras and generations from the pre-independent to the post-independent times. His story "Dinosar-ra Atma" ("The Soul of the Dinosaur") is a story that is based on the lost glory and grandeur of royalty and kingship in the post-independent era where a previous king finds himself like a dinosaur—a rare specimen of an extinct species.

But one cannot undermine the fact that one of the major features of Mohanty's narrative craft is humour—a humour that originates from his keen observations of the hypocrisy that exists in politics, in the false sophistication and lofty intellectualism in our academia. Some such stories that are the best examples of Mohanty's ability to create such humour in his writing are: "Rajadhani" ("The Capital"), "Vagabond" etc. where he thoroughly exposes and gleefully mocks at some of our follies and hypocrisies that we want to hide under the garbs of cultural and intellectual sophistications.

After providing a brief introduction to some of the important thematic concerns of Mohanty in the mentioned stories, I must now share with the audience some of my own experiences of translating Mohanty from Odia to English. It is famously said by eminent American poet Robert Frost that "Poetry is what is lost in translation"—a statement that is a clear indicator of how much difficult it is for the translator to carry the whole essence of the original text into the translated text. Each language is intrinsically embedded with certain cultural values and nuances specific to its own and which are perhaps untranslatable. Certain colloquial expressions, which Mohanty abundantly uses in his writing, are its best example. As a translator of Mohanty's novels and short stories, I have tried my level best to negotiate between two languages and two cultures that are, without even an iota of doubt, diametrically opposite to each other. It must be understood nevertheless that absolute faithfulness to the original text and the original language is an absolute impossibility.

Mohanty, in spite of his greatness and stature as a creative writer in Odia, can at times be accused of unwarranted verbosity though I do understand that a creative writer's creative process has limitless dimensions. Translating wordy sentences and expressions may look a bit challenging, but it is also a pleasurable experience to translate the clumsiness of certain colloquial or ornate and verbose expressions in the original language, i.e. Odia and re-present them in a simplified form in the target language, that is English.

At the end, I would like to thank my family members including my parents and my wife and friends who stood by me all through my effort. And at last my prayer to Lord Jagannath.

Sambit Panigrahi

CONTENTS

The Dance of the Ghost

While moving through the main line, there is a small station called Madhupur on the borders between Bihar and Odisha. I had missed the 64-Up and was waiting to catch 72-Up Madhupur Express and my travel-destination was the above-mentioned station. If the train was on time, it would have arrived at 7 in the evening. It was five more painstaking and strenuous hours of patient waiting for me. The waiting room was small, crammed and dingy and did not offer any conceivable note of joy or excitement for the waiting passengers whose crumpled faces looked cumbersomely sad, loathsome and haggard. Who comes to Madhupur these days? Its golden days are over and today it is an abandoned, forsaken place filled with stale reminiscences of a glorious but faded memory.

But in its heydays, lots of rangers from Calcutta and Patna visited Madhupur during Durga Puja or the Christmas vacations and spent happy and pleasurable times amongst its attractive and delightful natural vista, and amongst its warm, endearing and clement environment. Many of them, gotten enamoured by Madhupur's beautiful, temperate climate, its long, sprawling, green fields, its shady and succouring Sal forest and its adjacent, blue, and wavy Hazaribagh mountain-range, had constructed here attractive residential houses and palatial bungalows thereby converting the place into a marvellous, residential as well as holidaying hub. A huge rangers' colony was established in Madhupur due to the large and teeming influx of these regular and persistent vacation-time visitors and the place was particularly crowded by the swarming assemblage of these rangers' families during Puja and Christmas vacations. But these days, the new generation of affluent rangers travel to places like Srinagar, Darjeeling, Kalimpong, Goa, Calangute Beach, Mahabalipuram or Delhi to enjoy their vacation, being enamoured by the illusory grandeur of these big, honorific names. For them, Madhupur is no more than a deserted place, a forsaken slum.

Last year, I felt an irresistible urge to spend my vacation in Madhupur. I had a sheer and fascinating attraction for this place—an attraction that persisted in my memory like an awestruck adolescent's delirious fancy for a woman's body. Instead of staying in three-star or five-star hotels like these new generation of affluent men, I contemplated spending my vacation, quietly, inside an ancient, grass-infested, desolate building bereft of the gaudy flashiness of a furnished mansion. Madhupur's untraceable throngs of shifting shades and its intricate traceries of curvy and criss-crossing roads leading to the blue and wavy Hazaribag Mountains had mesmerized me, like unexplored spaces of an enchanting dreamland. A friend of mine had thankfully booked for me an antediluvian, dilapidated and moss-covered resort here where I thought I could comfily spend my desired days of queer and enjoyable holidaying. On a marble slab stuck on the resort's shabby and ramshackle gate, you could still find an unclear inscription written in Bengali: "Madhu Kunj."

After the first day of my stay, nevertheless, I was captivated by a feeling of intense boredom and depressive monotony. The place's empty and mysterious silence had in a way slaughtered the initial romantic buoyancy and exuberance with which I had arrived here with my excited mind pullulating with innumerable dreams, fancies and reveries about the place. By staying here, one could readily comprehend the difference between the tantalizing and illusory Madhupur glimpsed through the moving train's window-railings and the actual Madhupur lying out here—ashen and charmless—lousily outstretched across a swampy, abandoned wasteland. It is a clear and indisputable reiteration of the same, age-old distinction between illusion and reality—one a fanciful imagination and the other, a crude and unambiguous manifestation of irrefutable reality!

In the condensed evening fog, the distant mountains looked like hazy and cracked fences.

There were two ghostly houses lying adjacent to my resort and the third house after them was an old and antiquated one, inhabited by a retired judge. The overt expressions of antiquity overflowing across the grandiloquent but ramshackle texture of the house created an impression as if it belonged to an antediluvian, prehistoric era. The aged gentleman lived here alone. Of course, the only other beings living with him were a dark-coloured, imbecile-looking cook and a brooding dog whose reddish tongue dangled perpetually from his mouth like a spacious, rubicund curtain. Two houses away from his, lived an ex-landlord in a huge, palatial mansion. Like the retired judge, he also lived there alone, amidst throngs of memories—disjointed and hallucinatory—of his bygone days of affluence and might; those days had receded like fizzling-out waves of a plummeting ebb. He was certainly a mysterious creature; he never interacted with another human soul and was hardly seen coming out of his mansion.

Hotel 'Parvati' was the only place where you could fortuitously encounter a few ghostly human faces in the morning, in the noon and in the evening. If you looked at these people carefully, you could trace invisible masks of stoic indifference planted on their ceramic faces; they looked like weird and obnoxious-looking aliens from a distant, unexplored planet hovering somewhere untraceably in our vast, empyrean galaxy— the Milky Way. Engrossed in their own mysterious aloofness, they exhibited neither excitement nor exuberance.

*****

In the waiting room, I kept dreaming of so many fascinating things about Madhupur. While carelessly shuffling through a detective novel's pages, I sensed that a gentle lady sitting right in front and weaving a gorgeous woollen fabric threw at me strange, innocuous and stealthy glances, uninterruptedly. An urgent and outlandish curiosity flashed across her eyes like lightening flashing across a cloud-infested sky whereas a thin, sepia-tainted smile played on her lips like the exuberant spring's gentle, pacifying breeze. She was perhaps waiting there for an approaching train. I no more had the age neither did I have the youthful friskiness to enjoy a mature lady's ensnaring stare at me in such a calm, depressive and reclusive environment. At an age of above-fifty, my dishevelled, greying hairs flew over my head like sundry 'Kasatandi[1]' flowers undulating, with childish freakishness, across the vaporous and shimmering canvass of the steamy, drifty air. While shaving every day, I could spot on the brownish surface of the dust-infested mirror, a scourging army of deepening frowns ravaging across my blotchy and slackening cheek. It was a clear and irrefutable testimony of my dwindling youth and approaching old age. These frowns had freakishly intensified the skinny and wrinkly stubbornness of my ageing face.

The gentle lady kept on knitting wool with a downcast head. I kept shuffling through the pages of my detective novel.

*****

If I continued staying for two days more in that obnoxious haunted house in Madhupur, the proliferating aloofness in my acutely embittered mind would have snowballed into a deleterious ennui and would have driven me mad, without doubt. Two days ago, I met in Hotel Parvati a dreary gentleman who, despite his modest and ostentatious demeanour, looked to me like a thoroughgoing cynic; he curtailed my spirit by initiating a bizarre, depressing and tedious conversation with me and I had to listen to him willy-nilly, unwittingly. He was a local. I developed a casual acquaintance with him during that dull and not-so-exciting interaction over a cup of tea, and while talking, the gentleman smoked a branded, fashionable cigar and left out twisted, serpentine curls of smoke into the gloomy and condensed evening air. He told me: "With so many beautiful places around, why did you choose to come to this abandoned, swampy wasteland called Madhupur? Do you have a genetic strain of madness running across generations in your family? No sensible and well-meaning man ever comes for

---

[1]   It is a white-coloured Indian sub-continental flower.

holidaying to this empty and marooned place these days and an educated, well-meaning and well-informed person like you stepping into the dark crevasses of this abandoned Hell is beyond my honest comprehension. Have you ever come across, at least accidentally, these two rarefied and antique specimens of humanity—that judge and that landlord, these two self-obsessed, maniacal creatures? They hardly emerge from the ensconced spaces of their secluded chambers and interact with people around. Two local lads had once chivalrously ventured into the judge's house to collect some 'chanda²' for the Jagaddhatri Puja³." Wearing a multi-striped 'lungi⁴,' he hounded them out holding a large, terrifying stick in his hand."

Thankfully, I never visited this esteemed judge's abode for a gentle gossip, uninvitedly. But once out of an ad-lib curiosity, I had almost reached his building's entrance, unpremeditatedly, but was thankfully dissuaded by the repellent masses of weeds in his primeval garden and the ugly, scrunched face of that old, mossy and primitive building that giggled at me, spitefully, like a monkey. I came back hurriedly as if I had confronted a scary ghost.

The gentleman said again: "Didn't you find another resort other than 'Madhu Kunj'?"

I answered: "Actually, my stay in this bungalow was arranged by an old friend from Patna. I did not have to pay any rent except some meagre tips to the watchman."

"O! Engrossed in the gluttony of free accommodation, you have wilfully chosen to put up in this old, antiquated building bereft of the shiny freshness of a new and sophisticated, modern residence. But don't forget that after sunset, you won't confront a single soul loitering around in this enchanted landscape. Even, the old, local inhabitants of Madhupur, who are well-acquainted with every nook and corner of this locality, fear moving along its front road, once darkness sets in." The gentleman told in a shuddering voice, as if a dark veil of craven terror had enshrouded his scrawny, crumpled face.

---

2   Some monetary contribution.
3   A goddess in Hindu religion.
4   A long-clothed attire for Indian men.

I remembered how astoundingly the watchman had reacted that day when I handed to him my Patna friend's letter recommending my stay in 'Madhu Kunj.' I did spot a bizarre and obnoxious glare sweeping across his befuddled pair of eyes and could sense an uncanny strangeness floating fulsomely in his quaint and spooky response. He told in a sugary and kind-hearted voice that elicited the note of a highly sentimentalized, motherly concern: "Sir! If you confront any untoward difficulty or inconveniency whatsoever, please summon me, without the slightest of inhibition. I will be right up there at your service; in fact, I can stay in the bungalow throughout the whole night if you so wish. Sir, as you can see, this is an antique and forsaken bungalow containing nothing but a darkened void inside; I must not refrain from letting you know that there are multiple, weird and horrifying anecdotes floating in the air about this mysterious and enchanted bungalow. In fact, I myself have heard some of them from various mouths; they have sent scary waves of tremors and trepidations across my shuddering spine. That's why I am telling."

The watchman slept there on the bungalow's veranda during my prolonged and disillusioned stay of four nights in that marooned, sepulchral and obfuscated graveyard. He spent sleepless nights there in the brooding darkness, most of the time squatting on an old, decrepit bench at midnight while peering eerily into the shimmering darkness, without a thought, without a feeling. I often asked him out of effervescing curiosity: "Hey man! Why do you sit on the bench through the whole night instead of sleeping?" He answered with an unsolicited gesture of benignity: "Dear sir! Since you are a newcomer here, I am a little concerned about your safety, security and well-being in this godforsaken, deserted place. But you don't worry. I am always there for your help." I conjectured that the flooding deluge of sympathy that had swept across his pimple-ridden face like a spanning wave was for nothing but some handsome tips. I told myself: "Let him sit there for the whole night. What is my problem?""

I had asked that gentleman in Hotel Parvati: "Sir! Everybody is afraid of Madhu Kunj. Is it a haunted house?"

He had explicatively narrated before me the enchanting story behind Madhu Kunj's mysterious and esoteric conversion from a happy abode bustling with noise and vivacity into an enigmatic, haunted house overnight: "A few years ago, an old Bengali lady stayed here with her daughter-in-law and a few servants who performed their household chores. Both were widows. One day for reasons unknown, the daughter-in-law bolted the room from inside and committed suicide by hanging herself from the ceiling. After that scary incident's unfortunate occurrence, her mother-in-law departed for Brindavan permanently, and never returned. From that day onward, the house lies completely empty and abandoned; it has gotten converted into a frightful haunted house fuming with frightening wisps of gloom and darkness and nothing else. On rare occasions, of course, the mother-in-law's relatives do come and stay here for a few days and go back leaving the house empty and abandoned once again. A lot of people have confronted the daughter-in-law's ghost roaming across the area in ominous, moon-blanched nights, sometimes weeping and sobbing, sometimes laughing fiendishly at the occasional passer-by filling the empty air with its echoes and reverberations while at other times, singing a beautiful, melodious lullaby—a lulling, lethal death-trap. At times, she is found standing on the middle of the street, without a dress, stark nude."

But I must asseverate, proudly, that I never feared ghosts. So the story probably had very little perceivable impact on my unperturbed psyche and it was hardly able to fluster my unruffled temperament. But for a moment, I thought that perhaps this is why the watchman slept every night on the veranda with a lantern burning beside him, throwing innocuous streaks of gloomy rays into the blinding depths of the night—a night that wanted to devour it like a sharp-clawed and sharp-teethed, sinister beast. But again, I thought that he took that risk, camouflaging his own, innate fear of ghosts, only for the sake of receiving some handsome tips.

But does a human being live after his death? If no, then how could people witness that dead lady walking on the street, stark nude, in serene and clammed-up, moon-blanched nights? This was all rubbish, all rumours and unsubstantiated hearsays. I never believed in such puerile, moronic and airy ghost-anecdotes that are fundamentally unfounded, fanciful and misleading by their very nature. But the gentleman, while flicking the cigarette's ashes into the emptied teacup, said with an uncharacteristically grave and serious intonation: "Listen mister! You may not believe in such stories, and brush them aside by calling them sheer claptrap and balderdash. But don't forget that like some troubling and distraught memories that keep haunting us disturbingly, there are also some dead human beings that return into our midst as ghosts. Without being able to sever the sublunary ties with their previous births, they return recurrently into our midst as ghosts to relive their unfulfilled lives and to accomplish their unconsummated desires. Those that have been able to attain salvation do not, of course, come back."

"This is another mad man." I said to myself.

I did not argue further with the gentleman.

*****

I kept on shuffling through the pages of the detective novel in the waiting room.

But the gentle lady was caught unawares this time. She kept on staring at me, stealthily and was confident that with my attention overwhelmingly buried in my book's pages, I was not really catching her furtive and investigative glances directed at me and my calm, composed and unflustered countenance. But I did notice her nagging, clandestine activities, secretively and all on a sudden, lifted my head and looked straight into her eyes. Without being able to deflect her glance with an unanticipated suddenness, she was caught this time—unawares and red-handed. Then she gently smiled at me and said: "Can you not recognize me Nikhil Babu? You are Nikhil Chaudhury, right?"

I was stunned, flabbergasted. How could the gentle lady know my name? Did I have a previous acquaintance with her? The strange familiarity in her mature voice and the easy intimacy flooding across her cajoling stare thoroughly perplexed me in that little, embarrassing moment. The same deep chasm in her left cheek when she smiled!

I said impromptu: "Hey Kalyani! You are here. How strange!"

Kalyani was my classmate in college. During our student days, women's education had not flourished considerably. In our class, there were only a few girls, Kalyani being one of them. She said in a sullen and grumbling voice: "Ok! You did not recognize me, right! You all men are congenitally afflicted with this terrible malady called 'forgetfulness.' You do not take time to forget. You forget even your friends in a moment."

"A moment..." I snorted in the form of an instant and spontaneous response to her tenuous allegations. Then, I gently retorted: "Thirty-five long years are a moment for you, Kalyani!" and continued: "How could have I prognosticated that we shall meet here in this godforsaken, marooned waiting-room after so long? But how come you are alone? Where is your mister?"

A wry and dispassionate smile floated abruptly on Kalyani's lipstick-ridden lips and she said: "I have no mister, Nikhil. I am still Miss Kalyani Das, History Reader in Muzaffarpur Govt. College."

Now I realized that her sunken forehead was bereft of a dazzling vermilion mark, neither did she wear jinglingly flashy and elegant bangles around her wrist. There was also no decorative and embellishing golden necklace dangling around her neck, emblematic of a glossy and opulent married life. I mustered some courage and asked in a slightly apprehensive tone: "Is it due to some vow or for the sake of some spiritual pursuit, Kalyani?"

Kalyani answered promptly: "Well! You can say any of these. But you know pretty well that I was never interested in getting entangled in the abstruse intricacies of bothersome family life."

But how could she know that only for her sake, I had mugged up R. N. Tagore's poem "Kalyani" that day:

In the bower of flowers is thy matchless abode

O heavenly harbinger of beauty and prosperity!

Thou remain busy in your chores evermore.

I struggled to recollect the following lines; they were lost in time's circuitous labyrinth.

My friend Kuna parodied these lines and gleefully taunted me:
Alone is your abode in the midst of hawthorn fences.
Hey Kalyani! Thou remain busy in History Honours
class evermore.

Kalyani stopped knitting wool and started gossiping with me, loquaciously, digging out slaughtered memories from within the dark, dingy graveyard of time. She said to me: "I can see you have not yet relinquished your typical, juvenile habit of mindlessly shuffling through a book's pages. Do you remember that despite not being a History-honours student, you still frequented the Library to attend to History seminars? It was funny and intriguing for us girls. You used to open a History journal and hurriedly shuffle through its wasp-infested, yellowing pages; but I only knew that you didn't peruse even a single line. How could I have ignored the fact that you were actually a student of English Honours?" Saying this, Kalyani started chuckling at me, which within a split-second, turned into a loud and boisterous laughter whose echoes and reverberations were heard inside the waiting room's stuffy, obfuscated space.

Oh God! Kalyani observed my freakish, romantic ventures with such avid keenness and unsullied precision. I had absolutely no idea. But I was certainly Kalyani's diehard lover. But, of course, that love remained unexpressed and consequentially, unreciprocated. Firstly, I was a pathetically shy and introvert guy, and more so, our society during those days was meagrely considerate and permissive, particularly in the matters relating to courtship between adolescent boys and girls.

That is why I could never tell her with a softened, mellifluent, and cajoling intonation: "Kalyani! I love you."

I was lost in vainly scrambling through these discombobulated arrays of past memories; but I did realize, immediately, that it was not a viable occasion for such hollow, sentimental recapitulation of forlorn memories and a futile, imaginative re-enactment of bygone events and episodes of my life. Meeting Kalyani, perchance, after a prolonged gap of many years was no more than a mere, fateful coincidence, a fluke, a serendipity. We could not also have discussed our families, as we had none, neither were we keen on engaging in vibrant political discussions. If I was a student of History, we could have perhaps discussed a few important historical events and episodes.

But I was an English-Honours student and I won't deny, of course, that I used attend History seminars, regularly, only to see Kalyani, to lose my fidgety 'self' in the protracting depths of her cowering, curvaceous eyes, to have that rare, conceivable feeling of completeness in her cool, succouring presence in my vicinity. I could recollect, even now, how my yearning heart beat uncontrollably in that languorous afternoon, enamoured by Kalyani's sweet, enthralling beauty.

But my friend Kuna did notice my perennial inability to fall in love and taunted me: "Which girl will ever fall in love with a coward like you?" Amongst our contemporaries, Kuna was an illustrious and acclaimed lover. I had seen him regularly receiving blue-coloured love letters from an unknown beloved, perhaps an exotic princess from a faraway dreamland. At times, I got jealous of an adroit and unfailing lover like him who could make a girlfriend with the blink of an eye and I was such an ineffectual novice."

Kuna told me again: "How can a coward like you ever impress a girl?"

Of course, I was an incorrigibly shy guy and was not adept in such queer and quixotic ventures into the dicey and perilous amphitheatre of obsessive courtship. But I had not hesitated to ask Kuna: "Then tell me what can I do to impress a girl?" Kuna promptly answered: "You have to be a little glamorous, a little chivalrous as girls envisage glamour and chivalry as men's most rare, treasured and adorable possessions. If one day you can muster some courage and hold Kalyani's hand in yours and say: 'Kalyani! I love you,' she would definitely reciprocate, and reciprocate unhesitatingly."

But I asked Kuna with a quivering voice laden with a momentous concern and apprehension: "If she complains before the principal?"

Kuna responded a bit snobbishly: "There is risk in everything in life, my friend."

His words still reverberated in my ears like a distant echo.

The cloudless autumn sky tumbled into my eyes in white, translucent splinters through the waiting room's open window. A light, white cloud drifted along the sky like a fuzzy and disjointed memory from our unfulfilled past; I could see it navigate through the air, right in front of my eyes, like a torn-away piece from my disgruntled heart.

I asked Kalyani: "Oh! I forgot to ask you about your destination, Kalyani. Patna or Hazaribagh?"

She answered: "I am waiting for 77-Down-North Indian Express. I will be going to Durgapur. My uncle stays there."

I breathed a deep sigh of relief. It was already 4 o' clock. 72-Up Madhupur Express was set to arrive in the platform at 7 pm. Of course, if it was on the right time! Like the gentleman in Hotel 'Parvati' confronting the denuded lady's ghost on the streets of Madhupur in flashy, crimson and moon-blanched nights, I was now witnessing the ghost of my past dangling in the mid-air, right in front of me, like a hazy and indistinct apparition. In a whimsical recollection of my past, I tried to recapitulate the extent of my desperation for a little proximity with Kalyani, years ago, during those fanciful days of my failed romanticism! The sheer thought of it perplexed my mind. I wondered whether we are all mere, inconsequential playthings in the hands of unsurpassable destiny, worthless like clusters of trinkets and gimcracks. When time's fleeting background shifts, also shift our action, our thought, our behaviour, our whole life—a life that is a compendium of uncertainties created by the ever-shifting and whirling flux of time. This realization came to me abruptly, like a sudden denouement, an epiphany.

I was deeply engrossed in my quiet, outlandish philosophizations, when Kalyani readily interrupted and said smilingly: "I cannot control my laughter when I remember that day."

I answered absentmindedly: "Which day, Kalyani?" I muttered inaudibly: "Your and my histories are tragic ones, Kalyani. Of course, now, they might look comic."

But she had not forgotten that incident: "Why were you so

nervous that day, Nikhil? Your face that day . . . It looked so outrageously funny and clownish." Saying this, she started laughing puckishly again while looking at my face with a slanted and impish gesture.

"Nervous! When?" I asked in a curious voice.

Kalyani became garrulous and said: "You came that day to the History seminar and shuffled through the pages of an archaeological journal while throwing sporadic, stealthy glances at me in the midst of the seminar's noisy, bustling hullaballoo. Grossly terrified, you breathed so heavily that I could hear its reverberations from a distance. And then, all on a sudden, you ambled towards me with hastened steps like a wrecking tornado and I buried my face in the History book of Sir Jadunath Sarkar, while blushing in embarrassment with a downcast head. With a panicky voice that clearly lacked confidence, you asked for a pencil for taking notes and without lifting my head, I quietly handed it over to you while purportedly avoiding frontal eye contact with you. But I could readily sense that you wanted to touch my finger, instead, and in attempting that (which in my comprehension was a preordained one, and perhaps instigated by some adroit lover-friend of yours) you dropped the pencil on the ground as your hand was shaking viciously. Not being able to hold my hand, you left the place bearing on your face a glowering and morose disposition."

It was indeed Kuna's formula that I wanted to apply on Kalyani. I had strategized to press her hand in the guise of borrowing the pencil and then, profess my love with manufactured expressions of grace and easefulness. But it was an incredible disaster when it came to the actual performance; I was thoroughly discomfited and humiliated. If someone could portray my chagrin on stage, it had to be none other than the great Charley Chaplin. But of course, Kalyani's funny recapitulation and ludicrous narration of the episode after years of its actual occurrence looked hugely awkward and disconcerting.

I no more wanted to listen to her narration with its funny and preposterous nitty-gritty details. So, to divert attention, I said: "Oh! It's very hot and humid today. These people have not even placed a table fan here for the passengers. They boil inside the waiting room like cockroaches, lizards and frogs boiling inside the cauldron of the Shakespearean witches. It's a bitter irony that these railway officials barefacedly pontificate from the high altar of official and moral accountability, and deliver unending harangues in the name of passenger- amenity."

Even Kalyani could spot reddish tinges of discomfiture blooming on my face like red roses in a garden, and readily refrained from venturing into that incident, any further. She buried her head down and kept knitting wool as if there had never been a conversation between us, thus far.

A bell rang breaking the waiting room's silence.

The bearer dashed into the room and said: "77-Down North Indian Express is arriving. This is the second bell."

I was assured that the train would arrive at last.

Kalyani's soliloquies that had continued so far like the Phoenician sailors' endless navigation across the bluish firmament of an endless sea had come to an abrupt halt. After a few minutes of breath-taking pause, she suddenly extended her right hand towards me and said: "Please do a bit of fortune-telling, Nikhil. You were a great palmist, right?"

"I was of course practicing palmistry and mesmerism etc. those days as a hobby, as a strange fascination that was born out of nowhere. But how could you know that?" I asked Kalyani.

She said: "The way you boys loitered around us, we also kept track of your activities, man. More so, I had so many times spotted palmistry books in your hand. Were you a serious palmist or what?"

Without responding to her juvenile inquisitiveness, I quietly held her right palm in my hand and perused the lines with utmost care and precision—the lifeline, the fate-line, the wealth-line . . . But I had truly forgotten the finer arts of palmistry, of course, due to my lately developed disinterestedness in that art, and also, due to invincible time's murderous, all-effacing sweep through the hazy and unclear terrains of my fragile memory. Holding Kalyani's hand in mine was no more a delightful and exhilarating experience, as it would have been a few years down the line. I felt very cold and apathetic with the placid touch of her toughening, desiccated palm on which her greenish veins and arteries intercepted and crisscrossed in an imperceptible and mindboggling mess. It was rather a gruesome feeling of utter discomfiture that I felt in that touch; the brooding, depressing evening on the top of it made her presence dull, unexciting and wearisome. With a feeling of ineffableness, I left her hand and said: "I have forgotten palmistry long ago, Kalyani. Is it so that a human being's destiny is written only on his or her palms?"

I could sense that she was a little hurt by my words.

Now, the third bell rang.

Kalyani came out of the platform holding an attaché in her hand. A yellow vanity bag dangled from her left arm like an inchoate reminiscence from our hazy and irretrievable past that had mysteriously followed us through time's eternal, all-embracing flow. Then she said to me: "Ok! Bye! Who knows when we will meet again like this, suddenly?"

I also walked a little distance to say goodbye to her, as an officious marker of courtesy and gentlemanly sophistication. 77-Down North Indian Express waited for three minutes in the platform and left. After a few minutes of heart-throbbing commotion, the platform came back to a standstill, to its original stoic silence, to its calm and unperturbed tranquillity in the midst of the enormous drift of things around. Human faces poured in, diffused into the platform's smudgy, sepulchral space, collided and mingled to form a clumsy confluence of hazy and splintered faces and then dispersed around like disjointed, sordid images of the ailing modern men.

My train was to arrive two hours later. There was not even a tea stall in the platform. Absentmindedly, I walked alongside the railway track for some time, only to get rid of my nagging boredom and cantankerous monotony.

The afternoon-shade had gracefully descended onto a 'Palash[5]' tree, right in front. The tree looked to me like a female ghost, a denuded female ghost, like the one the gentleman in Hotel

---

[5]   An Indian sub-continental tree with beautiful red flowers. Its botanical name is Butea monosperma.

'Parvati' frightfully witnessed on the abandoned streets of Madhupur in moon-blanched nights. Now I was witnessing the denuded, fiery ghost of my past right in front of me, in broad, pervasive daylight. But it did not surprise me anymore, neither was I terrified by its sudden, freakish inception. The ghost grew bigger and clearer, taking an ugly and ferocious shape in the mid-air. It looked at me with cruel, pitiless and taunting expressions; it ridiculed me by throwing a flurry of indistinct banters and sarcasms; it tried to terrify me by flaunting its grisly, grotesque monkey face. But all in vain! I showed my monkey face too and giggled at her like a vengeful adolescent. But it was an interesting encounter indeed. I could have never forgotten that. With a quiescent and restful sobriety planted on my face, I kept walking.

The ghost kept dancing horridly in the mid-air...

The Miner

It was drizzling lightly.

Enshrouded by misty, white clouds, the bleary top of the Karo Mountain was half-visible. The bell of Bird Company's mine rang with an ear-splitting and raucous clang... It was 12 o' clock.

On one side of the railway track, Janam Murda sat on a coal and manganese powder-heap and kept staring at the front road with vacuous, unblinking eyes.

Janam Munda was an old man. If someone enquired about his age, he would respond offhandedly: "I don't know." But if one went on nagging ad nauseam, then he would say: "May be forty." But in all fairness, he looked no less than sixty. His unkempt hair had all turned bedraggled and grey. His eyes were horridly swollen and were continually watering. His flat nose-tip looked like an obnoxious lump of flesh accumulated on his dusky-complexioned face. On his dark face, the large nose looked clear and prominent and elongated outward like a sharp-edged sword. Around his waist was wrapped a piece of begrimed, dust-ridden mine-cloth and around his head was wrapped a similar smudgy, grey-coloured cloth like the worn-out residue of a putrescent turban. In the murky cavity between his ear and his head, was stuck a half-burnt cigarette with a darkened, haphazard tip. Francis Hansda had offered him a cup of tea and one cigarette in the Badbil market.

Francis kept instigating him that if he went to the Padre Sahib, he would offer him money, clothes and also will gift him a piece of fertile land. Janam Munda would spend the rest of his life in peace, prosperity and happiness.

"What nonsense!" Janam retorted with vehemence and continued: "I would never leave my "Bada Bonga[1]" like you. How many days would I live more? There is nothing more in my destiny. I would never leave my Bada Bonga."

Janam Munda was the revered headman of Karo village. He had two daughters—Raymani and Phulmani who brimmed with the splendours of full-blown youth and their dusky, scintillating bodies had become attractions for every youthful passer-by. Their sweet smiles flew through Karo Hill's ravines like swift, golden rivers gurgling and frothing while meandering languidly through the winding, rocky terrains of the mountain. Their faces glowed like the resplendent moon of the full-moon night while their dark, supple bodies resembled two dazzling effigies adroitly carved in granite by a dexterous stone mason. Janam Munda thought he would have gotten twenty oxen as 'sukhmu[2]' by getting his daughters married to two able-bodied Munda men. But perhaps that was not in his destiny fraught with poverty and irrevocable wretchedness. Now there was no use going to that Padre.

Clad in the overarching shades of the Sal trees, the grey road curved like a serpent sliding sluggishly through the mountain's rocky and curvilinear trajectory embracing distant places like Inginijharana, Jorda, Kouda and Banei. On that road ran innumerable trucks and jeeps flashing their luminous headlights on the colossal bodies of the giant and immovable hills that sat haphazardly, like antediluvian statues clad in the kimono of evening mist. At the back of the driver's seat, there stood the tribal girls holding the truck's railing in their hands. There were beautiful, wildflowers stuck on their heads; their lips were flooded with uncanny smiles and their dark, agile bodies were stuffed with the deluge and efflux of full-blown youth. In the jerky

---

[1] A tribal god.
[2] Bridal price. In many tribes it is customary that the bridegroom's family has to offer the bridal price to the bride's family. This is exactly opposite to the dowry system where just the reverse happens, i.e. the bride's family has to offer money as dowry to the bridegroom's family.

movement of the vehicle, their deft bodies undulated lavishly while flaunting the overflowing abundance of their shimmering youthfulness.

Janam Munda's daughters Raymani and Phulmani might also be moving inside a similar truck gliding ruggedly through the winding, gravely roads along a distant hill's rocky pavements. They were no more visible to Janam's blurring vision; neither did he elicit an urgency to see them anymore. They had become abominable miners in the greed of new sarees and costly perfumes; they had gleefully offered themselves to company sahibs and Punjabi drivers for the sake of money; they had compromised with their purity and dignity, unabashedly.

Janam Munda won't care if they went to Hell. How long shall he live more? He was being watched by Burubanga of Thakurani Hills, Birabanga of the Sal jungle, Nagera of the Kara River, Hasabanga of the lowland and above all, Rimilibanga of the whole forest region[3]. He couldn't have left them for the Christian Padre. Janam paid soulful obeisance to these gods by genuflecting on the ground and then touching his forehead on the same.

A lone and empty goods train came rushing in towards the Badbil railway-crossing from Jamda station while whistling vociferously. The engine emitted thick and condensed volumes of fuliginous smoke into the air; the smoke coiled like an airy snake and congealed spirally into the atmosphere's expanded, smoggy and frosty reservoir. The empty wagons were loaded with soil impregnated with ores; they were carried to the Calcutta Port from where they were exported abroad through the voluminous ships that dragged their giant, metallic bodies on the bluish surface of the sea like pestilential, untidy roaches. Gold and dollars flew indiscriminately into the company-owners' pockets in exchange; they relished with the plundered wealth of the soil and the forest, like bloodthirsty beasts relishing on the flesh of the slain preys. The consecrated soil which the tribal men worshipped as Hasabanga and the sacred hill which they adored as Burubanga

---

3   These are different tribal gods.

were now being excavated and looted by the foreign companies; they had become mere commodities and sources of heavy dividend for these obnoxious bunches of savage and importunate traders who meant only business, and nothing else. The green hill on which the jungle god Birabanga roamed in the middle of the night playing his flute was now blasted and excavated and was left as a barren, treeless plateau, bereft of the dense, green foliage overhead that enshrouded the pious, and consecrated soul of the forest like a soothing, velvety cover. The god Birabanga who blessed the verdurous soul of the forest awash with greenness was now being brashly sold in the inclement and 'whores-infested' bazaars of Calcutta like a cheap, inexpensive commodity. These modern, civilized interlopers had plundered everything—the consecrated soil, the beatific, 'fern-crowded' hills and Karo's exquisite natural environ where the gods of the tribe cohabited with their impassioned and dedicated devotees—the clean-hearted tribesmen. They had looted Janam Munda's dazzling, refulgent sweat, his pure and unadulterated tribal blood and also the pious and untarnished dignity of tribal virgin girls like Sunia, Kainta, Raymani and Phulmani. After everything had been outrageously plundered and looted, the hill and the land lay barren and forlorn in the midst of a treeless, shrub-less, marooned wasteland, from whose slaughtered body raised a twirling, greyish whirlwind of dust, like an ugly, evil spirit.

Raymani had eloped with a Sikh driver; Phulmani had become a prostitute in the Badbil slums while suffering from venereal diseases like Gonorrhoea and Syphilis. Janam Munda sat with an empty stomach on a manganese dust-pile near the railway-crossing, shed tranquil tears from his sunken eyes and looked vacantly at the cold unconcern of a blithesome sky that was tumbling on his head like a crushing weight from heaven. Janam Munda was not just a denizen of the Karo village, but also was a glaring symbol of exploitation and torture.

Wagons after wagons were loaded with Bird Company's manganese ore and with Tata Company's iron ore. They were dragged by the scraggy and destitute tribal men and women labourers and were finally clamped to the railway engine that yelled with an ear-splitting noise and emitted volumes of serpentine smoke into the air. Soaked with the poisonous smoke, the wild flowers stuck on the women' heads dried up and looked like crumpled, desiccated paper-made flowers whose dampened and greasy petals stunk malodorously rather than emitting a cool, succouring fragrance. And then came a sudden cloudburst; it drenched the women's bodies dripping with sweats; the sweats mingled into the pouring rain's torrential deluge. Their wetted breasts beneath their half-torn, semi-transparent sarees looked arresting and prominent and could not evade the predatory traders' ever-watchful, hungry and lustful eyes.

Oh God! So much of beauty! So much of hunger! So much of plenitude! So much of poverty! They were all possible in the dark, mining regions of Odisha.

Janam Munda wanted to get up and move. The Karo village was a long way from here; it glimmered like a tantalizing and distant isle in the flooding sunlight of the luminous sun. During the days of sowing and harvesting, the villagers worked in the corn-fields and during off seasons, they worked in the mines. Some of them managed to get jobs there whereas the others had to return empty-handed. But Janam, and in fact, all of Karo's villagers abhorred the mines for they thought that they were the places of exploitation and to work there was nothing but a sordid compromise with their dignity and self-esteem. That is why the mine-owners often had to outsource workers.

Of course, these days, the scenario was no bleaker and discouraging; it had changed dramatically and the mines had become attractive places to work. One easily got cut-price liquor from their canteens, cheap cigarette from the adjacent Badbil market, and inexpensive perfumes and low-priced, colourful sarees from the same place. That is why, these days the workers, instead of abhorring the place rather relished working there, out of their own sweet volition. Yet in places like Karo, Khendra, Dalki and Belkondi, some villagers still apprehended to enter into the mines' dusty, repugnant and malefic compound for certain irrational, unfounded, yet conventional prejudices. For them, whoever went there became an abominable miner. Some strange rumour ran in these tribal societies that the mine-owners slaughtered some workers and offered them to Burubanga, and chopped off others' limbs.

Last year, the whole region was terribly affected by drought. Whatever crops Janam grew in his small piece of land was all annihilated by the devouring drought's all-encompassing, diabolic tongue. His lush green field that once pullulated with crops dancing in the soughing wintry wind had now turned into a barren, desiccated and famished wasteland.

But today the contractor refused point blank that there is no work. Eating some scanty boiled rice in the morning, Janam came to find some work in Badbil; but he did not get any. Karo was a long distance away. Janam got up to move.

II

The liquor shop at the end of the Badbil slum!

It was the weekend wage-time for the miners as the next day was a Sunday and the mine remained closed. The road was flooded with drunkards merrymaking in the middle while singing vulgar songs and displaying obscene gestures towards the indecorous tribal girls accompanying them. There was a scuffle amongst themselves; their recklessness knew no bounds and was flaunted in the mid-road in the form of a loud, noisy and unpleasant hullaballoo. The obscenely dressed tribal girls accompanying them kept on laughing puckishly at their rascally show of rowdiness and by the next morning, the whole week's income was splurged. What was left was only one kilogram of rice, and nothing else. The importunate womenfolk had already reached to extract money from their drunken husbands; the roadside pulse-vendors had arrived with sticks in their hands; the trade union's hooligan had also reached the spot for his quintessential 'chanda[4].' A huge rambunctious, clattering crowd had gathered in front of the liquor shop as if to reinitiate a clangourous, drunken carnival there in the dark. Broken clouds had dispersed all along the sky like floating fragments of butter in

---

[4]   Colloquial term for fees.

un-churned milk making the latter look like a gigantic, pinkish, embroidered canopy in the faint, glimmering moonlight. The vagrant moon peeped through their fissures while hovering in the sky like a drifting, shining saucer. A few drunken men had already started their frenzied tribal dance beating tin-drums at the shop's dark and dingy backyard.

Man Singh Munda walked languidly out of the shop with an alcohol-bottle squeezed in his armpit's dark and sweaty cavity. He was not particularly enjoying the ruckus made by the unruly crowd on the gloomy, chequered open landscape outside the shop lying outstretched like a tattered and perforated dirty carpet. He only wanted to drink alcohol quietly in a tranquil atmosphere in the brooding darkness of the jungle, at a distance.

Somebody called his name loudly from within the crowd. Man Singh looked back.

A Gorakhpuri[5] hooligan came out flaunting his obnoxious, shadowy, wide, dust-ridden chest with enormous vainglory. He was a new recruit into the Company and was hired from outside to work as a professional bouncer. He wore a pair of torn and ragged black trousers dangling like the slender torsos of two wild trees and a dirty banyan around his chest. A square-shaped locket hanged from a black thread around his neck like an ugly, sinister design carved on a stygian, muscular body. His legs tottered under an alcoholic spell and he swayed languidly like a drunken bear when he walked.

That day Man Singh had gone there with a resolve to bring Phulmani back from that Hell. But she had employed this hooligan to beat him up. But Man Singh beat him instead for which the latter was seriously injured and was hospitalized. Being a strong and athletically built able-bodied man of the Munda tribe, Man Singh possessed the hideous strength of a tiger. Who could beat him up?

Today the Gorakhpuri Narayan Prasad wanted to take revenge. He started scolding Man Singh using filthy and un-parliamentary slangs.

[5]   From a place called Gorakhpur in North India.

Man Singh looked back and stared into the prolonging depths of Narayan Prasad's drunken, vacuous eyes for a moment, and then, threw a solid punch on his flat belly. Narayan tumbled onto the murky ground with a shriek that mingled into darkness like the surrounding jungle's low, indistinct whisper. Man Singh snatched Narayan's stick from his hand and lifted it into the air to smash his head. But the next moment, he threw it away with a disdainful gesture of condescension and vanished into the jungle, soundlessly.

An unknown wild flower's ambrosial fragrance spread through the atmosphere like an odoriferous smell emanated from the colossal jungle's lush, green body. A restless cuckoo sang mellifluously from within the enshrouding dense foliage of a nearby mango tree. Man Singh sat on a moon-blanched clearing on the roadside, leaned dolefully against a Sal tree and stared deeply into the mysterious quietude of the moon-light-bathed jungle.

This golden moonlight reminded him of Phulmani, about the Indar[6] festival of older days. This Phulmani! A contemptible whore! She is dead by now. But what is the use remembering her? Man Singh dispelled her intruding thoughts from his mind and started ruminating over his own past while taking large sips of liquor from the bottle. His eyes had turned blood-red and he felt a sharp sting of pain in his plaintive heart—a pain that started flowing though his swollen veins like injected doses of venom.

He remembered his village, and his thatched, mud-house that floated in his memory like the shadowy fragments of a fractured dream. He lived in the village named Dalki. They had a little house on a small hill at the village-end. Man Singh's mother had painted its walls with a lot of care... first a layer of grey soil, then another layer of black soil and finally a third layer of yellow soil. Above was a roof of tiles. During this time of the year, the house got surrounded by fields filled with a pullulating crowd of green popcorn plants.

---

[6] A tribal festival where men and women dance holding each other's hands.

Today, that house is broken and streaks of greyish and blackish darkness ooze out like droplets of blood from its battered and wounded body. Man Singh's father died in the battle in Assam where the Padre had sent him to fight the insurgents on behalf of the govt. forces. At the village-end, his mother placed a stone under a Sal tree as a dull, sublunary remnant of her deceased husband. Two years ago, she was eaten up by a tiger in the jungle into which she had ventured to collect some wild fruits. Man Singh put another three-cornered stone near his father's stone. In spring, the flowers fallen from the deciduous Sal tree enshrouded them all into invisibility.

Man Singh was lost in his thoughts...

III

Many years ago, Karo village celebrated the Indar festival with unbounded excitement and vigour. The Sal jungle was filled with reddish 'Palash' leaves that spread through the greenish canvass of the forest like a locomotive calligraphy. Drunk with 'mahulo[7],' the young men and women of Karo, Dalki, Khendra and Belkondi danced in concentric rings to the tunes of the drum's thumping sound and the flute's symphonic music, while clasping each other's hands in tight, passionate grips. When their feet got tired dancing, they eloped into the jungle in pairs holding each other's hands and clung to each other in tight, concupiscent embrace. And then they roamed like errant souls unleashed on Kara River's sprawling sandbank that stretched like an unfolded, white carpet rolling alongside the streaming river—the river of eternity.

The nomadic moon had soared high up into the sky like a golden-winged eagle. Today was the time for love, for merrymaking, for amorous togetherness, for unmitigated rampancy.

The long day ended with the approaching evening. The moon had risen deep into the sky as usual. Man Singh kept playing

---

[7] A wild flower blooming in the forests and fermented to make alcohol by the tribal people.

his flute while looking unabashedly at the streaming emptiness of the distant horizon. Phulmani kept dancing with the other Munda girls; their waists and shoulders were joined together like beads of an undulating string. They looked like a bunch of aromatic, wild flowers swaying randomly, together in gentle wind, tossing their decorous heads to and fro in a wavy, vermiculate tracery.

Man Singh stopped playing his flute for a moment, walked towards Phulmani, coiled his right hand around her slender, supple waist, dragged her closer to his chest and kissed her on her cheek. Phulmani smiled mischievously for a moment, gave a gentle push to Man Singh and ran into the jungle like a dark shadow gliding across the long stretches of the moon-blanched sand. In a moment, she congealed untraceably into the jungle's surreptitious depth; Man Singh followed her with the frantic desperation of a lunatic lover and spotted her near a giant stone. He clasped Phulmani from her back and lifted her into the air. Phulmani kept paddling her denuded legs in the air for some time with counterfeit gestures of resistance while at the same time getting enamoured by the sweaty smell of Man Singh's sturdy, macular body. She was getting arrested by the ensnaring hypnotism of the latter's hurried breaths. Man Singh placed Phulmani on that giant stone and said: "Hey Phulmani! The moonlit night looks beautiful. What do you say?"

Phulmani smiled impishly again without uttering a single syllable, slept for a moment on his bared, hairy chest, and started scratching its skinny surface gently with her sharpened, dye-ridden fingernails. And then, she ran swiftly towards the river bank, sat on a shallow stone-pedestal and kept watching the vagrant moon swim across the river's calm water like a dazzling goldfish.

In the gently soughing spring-wind, there was the intoxicating fragrance of the 'mahulo' flowers.

Man Singh told in a loud voice: "Phulmani! I shall marry you." His voice ricocheted from the stony walls of the surrounding hills and filled the empty nocturnal air with its thumping reverberations.

Listening to his words, Phulmani chuckled mischievously again and ran across the river bank into further depths of the forest. For a moment, it seemed as if she merged into the streaming river at a distance and flew across its curvy trajectories into the midst of the blinding mist and fog lying ahead, interlaced in an inextricable mess.

Man Singh searched for her for a long time, and finally traced her on the bank of River Kara, beneath a Sal tree. From a distance were audible the relentless beating of drums and the mellifluous songs of the Indar festival. Phulmani kept humming a similar song. Man Singh sat adjacent to her and asked: "What song are you singing, Phulmani?"

Phulmani did not respond at all and kept humming the song heedless of the latter's enticing proximity. She was like the moon-blanched Sal forest; she could be touched, but could not be fully comprehended. Holding her in his arms, Man Singh put a vermilion mark on her forehead expecting that Phulmani will reciprocate. But she did not do anything of that sort and ran away into the village without giving any desired response to his earnest propositions.

IV

The alcohol from the bottle was not fully consumed by Man Singh yet; he slipped the bottle into his pant-pocket, absentmindedly, and kept dreaming about a pensive past that kept on haunting him like an irksome ghost. He was still left with a week's wage. Lighting a cigarette, he headed back towards his village with unstable steps, accompanied by the pithy and condensed darkness that walked alongside like a friend, a companion. He wanted to be thoroughly drunk today, drunk to the lees.

But there was a time when Man Singh abhorred liquor to an extent that he did not even intend to touch the bottle; its very presence for him was repulsive, nauseating. He kept himself at an arm's length from the drunkards and did not appreciate the obnoxious practice of drinking at all. He also abhorred the mines to the extent that he never stepped into its filthy, repugnant and despicable premises. But the day when Janam declared that he won't give his Phulmani to him unless he offered him ten oxen as 'sukhmu,' he was left with no other choice but to step into the accursed, dusty terrain of the mines. With unrelenting hard work through prolonged days and nights, he accumulated pi after pi.

But perhaps it was not in his destiny to get the money.

That year the whole area was afflicted with severe drought; there was not a single drop of rain for months together. Every procured food items from the jungle including wild fruits and seeds were all exhausted. Some people still managed to get some more of them from the jungle and survived on them for a few days more. The Karo villagers usually did not go to work in the mines unless there was dire necessity. But this time, they were left with no option but to enter into its dreary and sepulchral premise that they abhorred so much and always looked indignantly at. But Janam Munda stuck to his manly vainglory and muttered to himself with a proud and intrepid heart: "It's absolutely fine if I shall die without a single morsel of food; but I shall never step into the dank and clammy premise of that monstrous Hell. I am the son of this forest. I am the son of this soil. I have lived here. I will die here."

V

Phulmani sobbed intermittently while sitting alone inside the house that resembled an abandoned dark cave, an abysmal pit. Above, there was a dilapidated roof made of broken brass and tin. And on the roof, were randomly placed broken bricks, stones, fractured bicycle-rims etc. such that it was not blown away in an abrupt, stormy wind.

Even the cruel and pitiless moon did not spare her. The inside of Phulmani's hut was awash with moonlight flooding from the sky and streaming onto the pebbly floor through the dilapidated roof's fissures. It fell on the rain-water-filled gutter and on the incongruous scrambles of rotten mosses all around and also on Phulmani's gonorrhoea-afflicted, sick body. While shivering in high fever, she felt as if the cruel and savage moonlight stabbed her on her belly; she felt like shrieking in excruciating pain, but all in vain.

These days she gets high fever every evening. The next morning, she re-freshens herself with heavy dosage of alcohol, laces her face with aromatic talcum powder, puts clusters of wildflowers on her wig and wears a dazzling, multi-coloured saree to attract the customers. Nowadays she roams with a six-feet-tall Punjabi truck driver who looks like a demon from Hell and drives a truck without license. He earns hundred rupees per day. Some days, he goes to distant villages like Noamundi, Chaibasa, Chakradharapur and Koida to transport goods from the company and comes back to Karo village in the blinding depths of the night. He meets Phulmani near the alcohol shop where both drink alcohol and eat roasted chicken in an adjacent 'dhaba.' Then he carries her into the dark dungeon of a hellish, abandoned hut where he makes love to her like a beast. He squeezes her tightly in the inescapable barricade of his sturdy arms and stinking chest, undresses her in mad desperation, licks her dusky, fleshy body with his devilish, salivating tongue dangling out like that of a rabid dog, eats morsels of her flesh with brutish delightfulness, and pounds her hard on a half-broken cot that creaks bizarrely every time he forces himself into her. Reduced into a crumpled lump of flesh in his beastly arms, Phulmani keeps losing her essence in that darkness, woven around her like a tortuous and entangling net.

Today that Punjabi driver has beaten her black and blue under the heady spell of liquor. He doubts of having contracted some venereal disease from her. But Phulmani did not cry for the pain of her body, but for the invisible scar that was festering gruesomely inside her mind, was gnawing her soul like an avaricious beast.

She remembered Man Singh Munda; his apparition floated before her eyes like an indistinct flicker of an image; she remembered their amorous moments of proximity during the Indar festival celebrations. She could have married him and have lived happily ever after roaming in the forest, living on the wild fruits, seeds, dancing uninterruptedly in the immense festivity of many blissful springs.

But that year a heavy famine grasped Karo; its villagers

had to go to the mines to get some work. Phulmani's sister Raymani went to the mine along with the villagers. Janam Munda admonished her time and again that in the mines, they slaughtered the labourers and offered them to Burubanga; they chopped of their limbs and threw them into the dark pits outside as fodder for Hasabanga. But Raymani didn't give a damn and went to the mines.

But Phulmani did not come with her. She waited for the day Man Singh gifted ten oxen to Janam Munda and married her.
VI

It was a dark and cloudy evening in Karo filled with the soft, cloying, aromatic breeze of the zestful and exuberant autumn. Phulmani boiled some wild bitter-potatoes in an earthen pot which Janam Munda had procured from the forest. But they never lost their bitterness even after repeated boiling.

Raymani came back from the mines and sat a little far away from Phulmani. Janam, drunk fulsomely with rice porridge, lied almost unconscious on a dilapidated cot under a gigantic, shady Sal tree. The trance-inducing fragrance of wild flowers emanated from the forest's mysterious, atavistic body had hypnotized all living beings into dizzy spells of an inexplicable frenzy.

But another fragrance emanated from Raymani's dusky body—delicate and awful fragrance.

Phulmani asked: "Wherefrom comes this sweet, soothing aroma, Raymani?"

Raymani started chuckling in a drunken voice while Phulmani kept staring at her— speechless, bewildered, flabbergasted. She did not wear that old, grubby and worn-out saree anymore and what she wore instead was a garish, flamboyant and red-coloured one. She had delightfully stuck ornate and resplendent blobs of sweet-smelling wild flowers in her wig and had laced her face with aromatic talcum powder.

Awestruck, Phulmani asked in a befuddled and flustered voice: "Wherefrom did you get these, Raymani?"

Raymani, while continuing chuckling frolicsomely, took out a small perfume-bottle from within her saree and handed it over to Phulmani, casually and languidly as if it was a small and negligible thing that she gifted her with easefulness and she possessed things which are more costly and precious. The latter held that bottle close to her nose and felt its honeyed, assuaging fragrance, deep within her craving, prehensile soul. She was delighted. Like a magician, Raymani took out a piece of scented soap and a mirror from within her saree and flaunted them before Phulmani's dazed and flabbergasted pair of eyes. Phulmani swooped onto the mirror within the flash of a second, snatched it from Raymani's hand and looked at her face, narcissistically, in the hot, reddish streaks of light gushing out from the blazing furnace and radiating across her dusky and resplendent face. She couldn't imagine she was so beautiful. Enamoured and beguiled by her own splendiferous beauty, she didn't even know when the hot, steaming water from within the pot had evaporated and the boiling bitter-potato inside it had turned into a dark, putrid mass of charcoal.

She asked again, with an urgent tone of clamant curiosity: "Wherefrom did you get these, Raymani?"

Raymani answered while laughing insolently: "The mine-owner gifted me all these. He has promised to give more."

The next day Raymani and Phulmani were found walking towards the mine, hand in hand, arm in arm, chuckling, laughing, and merrymaking while buzzing and serenading melodious tribal songs and lullabies.

From that day onwards, Phulmani has slept with many contractors and has been deserted by many, innumerable times, of course being priced for the wilful violation of her modesty and chastity. Man Singh Munda has managed to buy ten oxen and has come on multiple occasions, to Janam Munda's house asking for Phulmani's hand, repeatedly and earnestly. But each time, she has kicked him away showering on him throngs of scathing and vituperative tribal slangs.

Of course, today the times have changed. The mysterious allurement of the mines has also vanished. There are times when Phulmani craves, desperately, to run into her mud-house in her village Karo, and congeal into its fostering, life-giving darkness, like an affection-craving child congealing into her mother's spongy, absorbent, and consolatory arms. She wishes to drink the lurid, fragrant autumn breeze to the lees and pacify her parched and tormented soul with the mollifying and comforting embrocation of a reposeful and assuaging calmness. Long ago, she had brightened the greyish, lacklustre walls of her house with tinctures of resplendent colourfulness by smearing them in layers with black soil and red soil brought from distances. But today she is an accursed outsider, a filthy, abominable whore.

Phulmani looked at the gravelly road that stretched and coiled into the distant horizon like a winding arc. She got enamoured by its soothing invitation, as if it would carry her back into her cradle, into the blissful days of her joyful adolescence, into her dreamy and delirious past... The road led to her Karo village. But suddenly she felt as if it was filled with thorns and in a fit of tremor, she looked beneath.

Gosh! She was bleeding from her feet, profusely. Phulmani shrieked in terror and buried her face in her hands. The next moment, she looked at the road again, but did not spot a single thorn. She looked down at her feet; she didn't bleed at all. With the gradual recession of the nightmarish reverie, she got back to her senses and gazed insensately into the farthest limits of the sky overhead. She looked into its bottomless excesses of emptiness and felt as if her inside 'being' was morbidly empty, like the sky itself; it contained no feeling, no emotion, no sentiment, but only a chilling, marauding vacuum inside.

VII

The bell clanged in the mine-owner's house. . . It was twelve o' clock in the night. A ghostly calmness had percolated through the dark night like a snake's venom. The clouds had slowly accumulated in the sky and the peripatetic moon had leisurely waned in their midst like a golden bird waning in the midst of clumsy assemblages of enshrouding foliage. Drunken to the throat, Man Singh stood in the darkness outside Phulmani's house in the hope that one day she would accept him, that one day she would extend her dusky, voluptuous arms in a welcoming gesture to cuddle him, and he would fling himself into her inviting body in a momentous fit of joy and ecstasy.

But that day for him was a day of startling revelation. While anxiously loitering outside Phulmani's cottage awaiting an affirmative response from her, Man Singh Munda surprising heard her whispering to somebody and then suddenly bursting out into piercing and tumultuous peals of laughter in the dark. He crawled closer to the door like a stealthy leopard and peeped clandestinely through a little fissure to see the mysterious occurrences inside the chequered gloom of the cottage's dimly lighted, obfuscated space. But what he witnessed was beyond his wildest imagination. On the floor, lay that Gorakhpuri hooligan Narayan Prasad with his enormous limbs spread out against the floor like a felled tree's strewed branches. Phulmani slept lavishly on his chest and kept laughing maniacally as if being possessed by an uncontrollable whim, a strange and inexplicable delirium. There was not a single cloth in her body. She went on beating Narayan Prasad's chest with her relentless fists in a frenzied rhythm and started laughing obstreperously again, like a mad woman possessed by a ghost. A broken lantern with a cracked glass-cover lying abandoned at the corner emitted streaks of diffusive, dim lights into the room's overarching darkness; they made things sparsely visible to Man Singh. Two or three unlabelled, country-made liquor bottles lay scattered on the floor.

Narayan Prasad had not yet forgotten the nagging and excruciating pain in his bones caused by Man Singh's beating that day. He kept contemplating that one day he will finish him off if he got an opportunity and then, shall bury him somewhere inside in an abandoned pit in the mines. With clenched teeth, he shouted: "You Man Singh..." Hearing Man Singh's name from his mouth, Phulmani started roaring like a lioness and told Narayan Prasad: "You are a neuter. You are only a man of words. You come to me the day you kill him. Now don't show me your ugly, cowardly face and get lost from here."

It seemed as if there was no peace in Phulmani's life till Man Singh was alive.

Narayan Prasad boasted: "See girl! You will see how I shall

finish that man off. Every evening he returns from the Rungta market through the Thakurani Road. One day, I shall hide myself in a roadside bush with an axe in my hand, and shall finish him off in one stroke."

Narayan Prasad started roaring like a lion.

Listening to Narayan Prasad's words, Man Singh's blood coddled like sizzling hot water sloshing fiercely inside his throbbing clusters of veins. Without wasting a minute, he gave a solid and thunderous kick on the door; it opened from inside with an ear-splitting bang. Looking at Man Singh's violent, monstrous figure materializing ominously right in front, Phulmani shouted: "Man Singh! You go from here. Otherwise, I shall call the police." Without uttering a single word, Man Singh rushed, hysterically, to the corner of the house, picked an axe lying out there and stood before Narayan Prasad and Phulmani while staring at their aghast and frozen eyes with the unmatchable vengeance of a wounded tiger. Narayan Prasad understood the gravity of the situation and intended to tame Man Singh by jumping onto him and capturing him promptly in the barricade of his sturdy, muscular arms before the latter could do anything outrageously fatal. But before he could do anything, Man Singh severed his head in a single, monstrous blow. Streaks of fresh blood were splayed all along the floor and a few slashes also fell on the dimly flickering lantern's cracked, dust-infested glass. While screaming, Phulmani tried to rush out of the house, captivated by the craven terror of imminent death standing right in front of her in the form of Man Singh turned into a bloodthirsty demon. But before she could escape, Man Singh held her by her hair, threw her on Narayan Prasad's body and cleaved her head into two halves with another blow.

With two severed heads in his hands, Man Singh surrendered before the police.

VIII

It was raining cats and dogs that morning. The rain did not stop at all. It was a dampened, swampy and cloudy Sunday. The mines were closed.

Janam Munda kept ambling errantly across Kara River's banks while catching glow-worms. He had not eaten glow-worm curry for a long time. When his daughters lived with him, they used to bring a lot of these to make tasty and delicious dishes for him. Janam Munda used to salivate looking at the seething congregation of these glow-worms in the air.

He had already placed folded Sal leaves near the anthills' holes. Within a blink of his eyes, these folded leaves were filled with hundreds of glow-worms. The clouds thundered intermittently over the Thakurani Hill. Kara River's darkish waters brimmed with great profusion and rushed towards the sea, towards eternity.

Somebody shouted from behind: "Hey Baba! Hey Baba!"

Janam looked back. Karkanda Munda of his own village was running frantically towards him. He worked in the Badbil mines.

Karkanda reached near him gasping vigorously and said in a breathless voice: "Phulmani's body lies there in the police station. Go and bring her. Last night, Man Singh has murdered her along with that Gorakhpuri hooligan, Narayan Prasad."

Janam looked at Karkanda's face—dumbfounded, flabbergasted; then, he kept looking at the Thakurani Hills like a thunderstruck lunatic. He had forgotten catching glow-worms.

IX

It was customary in the Munda tribe to cremate the body. Phulmani's pyre was slowly getting extinguished by the gently blowing breeze on Kara River's banks. The darkening clouds kept accumulating in the sky in throngs and clusters. On the brimming waters of the river, Phulmani's funeral fire danced elatedly like the jungle's daughter Phulmani herself.

Janam Munda looked at the Thakurani Hill at a distance and ruminated: "I have lost everything. What else remains here?"

He thought of leaving the Karo village. But where would he go? Singhbhum? That was also a place full of mines. Banei? It was also the same there. Pallahada? Would the contractors have left any jungle uncut there? Who knows?

Janam Munda knew it right. Whoever goes to the mines, never comes back. Burubanga kills him or her by sucking their blood. If you disrespect Burubanga, would he not kill you? He could not imagine why his Phulmani and Raymani chose the path of destruction? Janam looked at the jungle again. There were times when the peacocks danced in this forest and tigers roared from distances... There was a time when Burubanga roamed here in the depths of the night playing his flute and everybody listened — the mesmerized forest, the dumfounded trees, the dancing peacocks, the passing clouds and the astounded moon — everybody. Now in the depths of the night, one hears only the hellish sound of axes cleaving through the throbbing, terrified hearts of trees that were turning into insipid, dead pieces of wood. The land is plundered; the hills are destroyed; his Raymani and Phulmani are gone. Before that, he had also lost his wife. Tears jerked in his eyes.

Phulmani's pyre was completely extinguished now. Janam collected a handful of ashes and a few pieces of bones from the ash-pile as the last surviving remnants of his dead daughter, and kept walking towards his village while a calm and unflustered expression of an angelic stoicism had precipitated onto his stiffened, metallic face, quite visibly. There was no emotion left in his heart. It was dry, dispossessed.

The next day, he dug a hole near his dead wife's grave beneath the Sal tree and filled it with Phulmani's ashes and bones that he had gingerly collected from the ash-pile. Then he lifted a shining, three-cornered stone and placed it on the hole. A few Sal flowers fell on the stone like tear-droplets from his eyes.

Janam Munda believed that this old Sal tree is Burubanga's consecrated abode. But the savage contractor has already marked it with tar. In a few days, it would be felled by his axe. Janam prostrated on the ground, paid obeisance to Burubanga, and then started walking in an uncertain direction, away from the tortuous saga of plunder and exploitation of the civilized world. While leaving, he looked once at his wife's grave and once at his old, dilapidated hut. In his blurring vision, the road stretching ahead looked to him like a dark, desiccated and waterless river — the river of time—meandering languidly into the misty depths of the frosted horizon—the horizon that is nothing but a thrown away fragment of eternity into which everything dissolves—desire and memory and this filthy, decaying body. Janam had no idea where his own grave would be.

He wiped out tears from his eyes. Trucks after trucks kept racing towards the Koida mines. Janam kept trudging into the unknown depths of the jungle...

A Moonlit Night in Spring

It was already past 12 o' clock in the night. Hrudaya Babu was still not able to sleep even after consuming two 'calmpose' tablets. No! They did not work anymore; they had become totally ineffective. A little while ago, the sound of a drunkard's moving feet was faintly audible from the empty road. . . Certainly, he was returning from an alcohol-club; his feet moved unsteadily, sometimes to the left, sometimes to the right making a low, clattering sound that dissolved in the darkness like a distant, unclear music. That sound in the tranquil night reverberated in Hrudaya Babu's mellowed ears and disturbed his sleep, periodically. He felt at least something worthwhile was happening in his otherwise dull, companionless and uneventful life. At least, there was a living human being in his vicinity and this feeling infused some kind of a reinvigorating and buoyant spirit into his otherwise sterile, desolate and woebegone heart. The sound slowly dissolved in the quiet night like a dissoluble pill in a glass of water.

Outside, was spread the spring night's crimson moonlight like a golden sheet enshrouding the darkened Earth, that was lying out there, across the dark night's sprawling space, like an abandoned corpse. Through the right-side window, a lurid splash of that light fell scattered on Hrudaya Babu's wide, spread-out chest. A portion of it was also spilled on the empty bed, incongruously diffused into its floridly embroidered coverlet.

Time is very strange... One day this beautiful moonlight ignited fire in Hrudaya Babu's excited nerves and tendons combusting them in the flames of desire. Even today, it rejuvenates his mind and spirit despite his sick body, his approaching old age and his proliferating infirmity. The same moon light, the same spring night, the same hypnotizing south-wind! That day, this moonlight became a dazzling ornament on the soft, sensuous body of Hrudaya Babu's bride and filled his mind with irrepressible, youthful vigour and vitality. But now she has grown old and feeble, and has taken customary recourse to compulsive spirituality. She spends most of her time in 'Puja'[1] and other spiritual activities inside the worship-room and once on bed, she starts chanting God's name relentlessly till sleep descends into her eyes like the former's heavenly blessing and closes them down with its soothing, assuasive spell. At times when Hrudaya Babu gets a little naughty and sleazy with her for a change, what shrilling, cacophonic and repellent sound she makes!

"Shameless fellow! Characterless fellow! Get lost;" she shouts.

Thank God! These days, she is on a leisurely pilgrimage to Puri, to bathe in the sacred sea, and to see Lord Jagannath's holy face and to stay happily immersed in her phantasmagoric, spiritual world. She is there for the last two days, and expectedly, would spend a week there. And for Hrudaya Babu, this week is supposed to be one of unbounded freedom, of enjoyable freakishness, of quizzical ventures. But what great adventure could he have ventured into with the meaningless freedom of this arthritis-ridden, frail body? He could only look at this ticklish moonlight of spring with gaping eyes and ruminate over his lost, days of grandeur and romanticism...

But still, this short-lived freedom, this profligate liberty is alluring and attractive. Now he does not have to worry about his wife's trenchant admonitions: "Take medicine on time." He no more has to fear the irksome ghosts of diabetes and hypertension. He does not have to read *Geeta* or *Bhagabata* compulsively sitting on his wheel chair; neither does he have the coercion to sit beside an obnoxious 'Baba' caught from somewhere by his wife and bow to the strange and bizarre rules laid down by him. There is no shout from his wife, neither is there any screeching, ear-splitting

---

[1]   Worship of any Hindu god or goddess.

allegation of being a shameless, characterless fellow by her when he sits restfully with his whiskey bottle on the chair.

But on the contrary, this aloofness, this alienation is also a torment. There is some satisfying sense of companionship even in a skirmish with the wife; there is a gratifying feeling of completeness even in this acute and deteriorating conjugality. After Surama Devi has gone on pilgrimage, a terrible sense of loneliness has completely captivated Hrudaya Babu like a conjuring spell of hypnotism cast on him by a wicked magician.

This moonlit night of spring! This fickleness of this south-wind! This lifelessness! This aloofness! And this paralysed body! Hrudaya Babu felt a sharp sting of pain in the inmost recesses of his soul.

Vexed and agonized by the pangs of aloofness, he took out a cigarette-case from beneath his pillow and tried to light a cigarette. These days he finds it difficult to light one, alone by himself. The fickle gushes of wind barging in through the window like unwelcome trespassers extinguished the matchsticks once they were lighted. After trying hard for many times, Hrudaya Babu finally succeeded in lighting a cigarette, inhaled a mouthful of smoke, and then, exhaled some of it bearing a stoic, concocted expression on his face. The smoke coiled into the atmosphere in an exquisite, circular trajectory and looked like a white spectre, carved in the air, against the crimson canvass of the moonlit night. Hrudaya Babu felt like conquering a hitherto unconquered mountain range.

Who shall believe that during his younger days, Hrudaya Babu was a tireless hunter? Who can imagine that he roamed through the mountains with a rifle in his hands, day in and day out and spent most of his life in the jungles and hills as a forest-conservator?

In the immense tranquillity of the night, the sound of someone's footsteps kept approaching his vicinity through chequered gloom of the garden. No! It was perhaps an illusion, the semblance of a sound —he thought. A few street dogs roaming helter-skelter barked vigorously into the labyrinthine depths of the night. Listening to their bark, an Alsatian dog in the neighbourhood reciprocated and barked with equal vigour and savagery. It barked for some time and then, stopped while everything became quiet again.

Hrudaya Babu regressed into his past laden with roiled assemblages of wistful and morbid memories coupled with exultant and happy ones. With the abject sterility of this paralysed body, he could not imagine that one day he possessed a joyous and exuberant youth, that one day he could dream of impossible things and could achieve many of them.

Those days, his nights were spent in the empty, marooned bungalows surrounded by the dark, ubiquitous and pervasive forest. But even once, he didn't feel the pangs of aloofness in the brooding and vicious emptiness of his surroundings, quite astoundingly though. The forest's beauty had mesmerized him. The golden deer's luscious eyes had maddened him into an interminably seductive frenzy.

But Hrudaya Babu could not write a single poem in his life. He had tried many times; but he never liked his own poems. He could never captivate his heartfelt feelings correctly on pen and paper, by adorning them with multitudes of decorative similes and metaphors. Hrudaya Babu kept on tearing off and throwing away his poems, one after another, every now and then.

But still, he has always remained a dreamy, romantic, and poetic mind.

Caught in the maze of multitudes of divergent, embroiling thoughts, Hrudaya Babu suddenly spotted the blurry and darkish silhouette of a human head outside his window; and was shaken from inside at the sight of such hazy and bloodcurdling spectacle. He got up with a jerk. Though initially he did not comprehend much of the frightening proceedings in the garden's dark and muddled environment, he could sense immediately afterwards that the man was actually cleaving the grill-wires with a cutter. Its sound was faintly audible.

Hrudaya Babu understood instantly that this man was either a thief or a dacoit. It was no use calling his servant Mangulia as he usually slept deep, like a modern-day Kumbhakarna, and hardly responded to his call despite its unmatchable vociferousness. He required a fire-brigade bell to get up from sleep. Hrudaya Babu conjectured that he must have smoked opium and fallen deep asleep somewhere, having gotten comatosely inebriated by the intoxicating spell of this narcotic material. He attempted to pull out his revolver from below his bed, but quickly remembered that it was not loaded. Surama Devi was always appallingly discomfited by the awareness of a loaded revolver's sheer presence beneath the bed-cushion. Then what was the use of keeping a revolver? But she never understood the logic; neither did she try to understand.

By this time, the man had entered inside the house by cutting the window-grill.

Hrudaya Babu switched on the bed light and in the electric bulb's faint glimmer, could see a dark and moribund silhouette materialize into an ugly and gruesome human figure, right in front of him. He first got terribly scared, but then regained his composure due to his vast experience and his lately cultivated indifference and stoicism towards life. The man wore a short, worn-out black pant; his wide, open chest was filled with wavy, undulating hairs and a quadrangular locket hung inchoately from his neck by a crummy and greasy black thread. He had a huge and curly black moustache coiling below his nose like a dark, venomous snake and a dirty handkerchief circled around his head like a dark, smudgy cover enshrouding an abandoned corpse. Hrudaya Babu thought that the man is a new recruit to the profession of larceny.

The man was also startled to see Hrudaya Babu right in front. He might not have expected someone in the house to be awake so late in the night. Hrudaya Babu thought: "Let him loot and plunder whatever he likes. I don't have the strength to stop him. But let me at least enjoy a man's relishing companionship in the midst of this brooding and tortuous aloofness.

Hrudaya Babu told: "Hey man! Sit here. Why do you get so desperate? I am giving you the keys of this steel cupboard. You do not need to take out your knife or something and threaten me. You are actually the rich people's friend. But unfortunately, they call you a dacoit. You take comfortably whatever you want. But before that, come and sit with me and help me light my cigarette. Let's sit down and talk. Do you fear I will call the police? See! The telephone lies there, dead, at a distance. Moreover, I am a disabled man. So, you need not worry. Please sit on that wheel chair. There is no other chair nearby."

That man was shocked and flabbergasted to hear such kind, friendly and compassionate words from a house-owner, at the backdrop of such an unusual and unexpected encounter. Then he sat quietly, as per the latter's endearing instructions, on the wheel chair without uttering a single word. Then he lighted his own cigarette and also Hrudaya Babu's.

On the road, a speeding car almost met with an accident. In the indistinct gloom of the night, it would have crushed into the roadside sewage; but the driver put the break right in time. But the rugged creak of its wheel rubbing against the scabrous and bumpy soil was largely audible through the night's immense and deathlike tranquillity.

The man suddenly got up from the chair, took out a knife from his pocket, brandished at Hrudaya Babu and said in an aggressive tone: "Keys..."

Hrudaya Babu said in an unruffled voice: "Keep that knife in your pocket, friend. I told you don't need to brandish your knife or anything at me. The keys are with my wife who is now in Puri. See below the pillow. There might be a duplicate key"

Heedless of Hrudaya Babu's words, the man kept on brandishing the knife uninterruptedly at him, inserted his left hand below the pillow and extracted the duplicate key dangling from a dazzling, metallic key-ring making a faint, jingling cadence which clashing against another key in the same ring. Then he opened the steel cupboard and went on scrambling through the racks with both hands, desperately, like a moonstruck lunatic. There was no other thing in the brief case except a few crumpled, neglected, wasp-infested, dust-ridden papers.

Yet, there was no sense of fear or apprehension on Hrudaya Babu's face; rather he thoroughly enjoyed the scene and relished its preposterous farcicality. In the meanwhile, the burglar kept on examining two fixed-deposit forms in the dim light. Hrudaya Babu said; "Hey friend! You will get bundles of currency notes in the steel cupboards of ministers and leaders. They don't keep them in banks to evade income tax. But all our money is in the bank. Those two pieces of paper will be of no use for you. Those are fixed deposit forms."

The burglar threw the forms on the ground with a visible expression of disgust and indignation, and went on scrambling desperately for something more in the shelves and in the brief case. To his greatest delight, he discovered a gold necklace and two finger-rings inside the brief case; his incisive, razor-sharp eyes lit up with blistering excitement.

Hrudaya Babu told: "Friend! If you kindly spare that necklace, I will be greatly obliged. It is my younger daughter Sujata's. She is now with God. I had bought it for her the day she first went to college, elatedly, and stepped into its premise with lots of joy and excitement. She used to go there wearing this necklace, with a happy and contented disposition markedly visible on her face; she relished wearing this necklace."

Reminiscing his dead daughter, Hrudaya Babu drew a huge, voluminous breath into his lung and paused for a moment like a lifeless effigy, with its stone-carved eyes looking pensively still and immovable. Then, he stared into the nocturnal, moonlit air with an expression of consummate stoicism; within a moment, his stare decocted the night's self-indulgent, juvenile fickleness into a maturely grievous expression of intense grief. By that time, the man had splayed the whole floor with almost all of Surama Devi's costly sarees from the cupboard, and with some of Hrudaya Babu's elegant and gaudy ironed dresses. The gold necklace and the finger-rings had by that time slipped into his pant pocket.

In the bedroom's dim blue light, one vodka and two whiskey bottles dazzled flickeringly in the cupboard's polished and glistening shelf. The man had already taken out the vodka bottle, but Hrudaya Babu told: "Don't bring that one, my friend; I don't have tomato juice and there is no soda either. If they were there, I would have made excellent bloody-merry cocktail for you. Even today, I am known for making excellent cocktails, my friend. Rather you bring that whiskey bottle. It can be drunk with water. This is not your cheap, country-made liquor. This is sophisticated foreign scotch. It's the customs thing, you know."

That man held the Vat-69 bottle in his hand and sat on the sofa, heedless of Hrudaya Babu's continual interactions with him in the form of an amicable and friendly chatter.

Hrudaya Babu told: "The adjacent room is the dining hall. Please take a little trouble, my friend and bring two glasses along with one water-bottle."

The man obliged unhesitatingly.

He hurriedly poured three pegs of whiskey into the glass and started drinking them in the mad desperation of a terribly thirsty man. Perhaps, that is how he drank his alcohol— to gulp large pegs at one go, without even water. Presumably, he was not accustomed to measured pegs and did not require water at all for drinking his alcohol. He finished off the glass in a single breath, and then lighted a cigarette. Hrudaya Babu, contrarily, poured a peg of whiskey, and then some water into his glass, and then, started sipping from it in smaller gulps.

Hrudaya Babu said: "The flavour of scotch is different my friend."

Next time, the man poured a lot more into his glass, leaving perhaps only one peg in the bottle.

But suddenly, they heard from the road frequent, screeching whistles from the patrolling police van rambling through the condensed dark of the night like a giant, nasty vermin. The man became aghast and serious and got worried out of fear and a note of momentary, panicky apprehension floated on his face, and then precipitated into an inchoate cluster of furrows and frowns. As per recent newspaper reports, some 'khalistani[2]' terrorists had encroached into the city, and the police were frantically searching for them in the suspect area. The combing operations had intensified of late, and was supposed to continue ad-nauseam till dawn.

The man switched off the light.

Hrudaya Babu still kept on relishing the man's proximity, even though he was purportedly a notorious burglar. For a long time, he had not enjoyed anybody's gratifying and heart-warming

---

[2] The Sikh terrorists of Punjab who wanted a separate land form them known as khalistan.

company, over a few pegs of whiskey, in an amicable, unselfish conversation. He hardly had occasion for such intimate one-to-one interaction except with specialist doctors over his persistent and chronic medical conditions.

With a whiskey-filled glass in his hands, Hrudaya Babu's auspicious night-friend had become completely oblivious of the former's presence in his vicinity. Perhaps he felt a little uneasy, awkward and discomfited in the house-owner's presence.

"The man doesn't know how to talk in a decent and relaxed manner"—thought Hrudaya Babu, eliciting a little not discontent on his expressive face, particularly because of the man's dull, sterile and stubborn unresponsiveness to his words. In single gulps, the man had finished off large pegs and then, had started casting his avaricious and predatory eyes rapaciously on the other bottle lying forlorn on the cupboard's gaudy and glittering shelf.

Hrudaya Babu told him: "Quickly change your black short pant, 'night-friend.' I know you won't reveal your name to me; so, I call you 'night-friend' without any decent and proper name of yours available to me, right at the moment. Now if you venture outside with this tarnished short pant, this foreboding pair of dark glasses and with this gigantic, bull's figure, then you will encounter the real danger. People might think you are a dacoit. That's why please obey my instructions. Please change your dresses."

The 'night-friend' wilfully obliged. He kept the whiskey glass on the table and changed his dresses quickly.

Hrudaya Babu emitted another mouthful of smoke into the air and said: "That's better. You now look like a thorough gentleman imbued with refined and modern etiquettes. Ha! This figure! These so called gentle or savage figures! All are tailor-made. Your attire makes you either a gentleman or a savage. Now if someone spots you in this renewed apparel, would he ever imagine that you encroached into my house as a plunderer, in the blinding depths of the night, by cutting the gate's grills? Now you look either like a sophisticated leftist intellectual or an accomplished artist, 'night-friend.' Cheers... ."

Now, the 'night-friend' responded, and responded with a surprising note of impeccable vehemence and authority. Breaking the dark night's inglorious monotony, he spoke in a grave, whiskey-drunken, and inebriated voice: "Ha! For your kind information, I am a postgraduate from a university. M. A. in Political Science... Yet, I am unemployed, jobless."

Hrudaya Babu responded in a taunting note of sarcasm: "Then you must have cleared your examination through malpractice. Right?"

The 'night-friend' retorted angrily: "So what! That is the universally acceptable practice everywhere today. You pass the examination either by malpractice or through some other connection. But my certificate is genuine."

The 'night-friend' continued: "I have appeared in many job interviews, but could not succeed in one. I remained unemployed for long. Then once I heard a minister pontificate in one of his inspirational harangues that our young men should invent their own ways and means for self-employment in a scenario where the government is not able to generate adequate employment opportunities for them. I got inspired and discovered this potent method of self-employment—burglary. Now this is my career, my illustrious career."

After telling this, the 'night-friend' inhaled a long, deep breath, and sat on the sofa flaunting a gesture of casual heedlessness on his face.

Hrudaya Babu remained speechless.

The 'night-friend' went on: "But you disappointed me a lot, my friend."

Hrudaya Babu enquired: "How? How did I disappoint you after offering so much of congenial and affable hospitality?"

The 'night-friend' answered: "After specializing in grill-cutting, I came here with the thrilling anticipation of plundering lots of wealth. I had gotten prior information that that you are suffering from paralysis and you spend most of your time being seated on a wheelchair. Your pious, devoted and world-renouncing wife is on a pilgrimage to Puri. Your servant is a perennial and compulsive opium-addict. The myth that floated in the air about you is that as a retired forest-conservator, you have amassed lots of wealth inside your gold-stash buried in some unexplored, secluded corner of your house. I had imagined that the plundered wealth from the forest's womb, from the infinite riches of Nature's bountifulness lies concealed somewhere, like a dark and unexplored secret, inside your stuffy and grandiloquent house. But whatever little I find here is just chickenfeed. You don't have a sandal-wood cot in your bedroom; neither do you have expensive jewelleries hidden in your gold-stash. Or is it your strategy, your witty shrewdness? Have you dug your wealth somewhere else to befuddle burglars like us? Does a dacoit burgle into someone's house in this blinding night's opaque darkness to engage in a gentle and cordial conversation with the owner over a few pegs of whiskey? To exchange pleasantries? Nonsense! My whole night is spoiled."

The night-friend tucked an addendum to his little harangue and said: "After my ceremonious entry into the profession of larceny, I had never confronted such terrible disillusionment in my life. Encroaching into your house, after the accomplishment of an arduous and painstaking grill-cutting exercise, looks to me an absolute disaster now.

Hrudaya Babu extended his heartfelt commiserations to his night-friend and answered: "You trust me, my friend. Whatever I may be, I am not at all shrewd, cunning or duplicitous in my demeanours. I kept on hunting through the forest all my life. When the hunter and the beast confront, no shrewdness works, my friend. Either you kill it or it will kill you. My whole life was spent running after the mysterious, feral animals of the jungle. I was enchanted by the enigma of the forest, my friend, by its splendiferous beauty, by its incandescent charm. I spent all my time, all my life pursuing the forest's unrevealed secrecies, its unending expanses of abstruse and mindboggling mysteries. How could I then have made for myself sandal-wood cots? Then also my friend, we are people of the older generation. We are not adept in this nasty and abominable craft of stealing. We filled the forests with sandal-wood plantations. Now these wood-mafias smuggle them, and sell them to the corrupt govt. officials who make expensive cots from the smuggled timber."

Outside, the sound of the patrolling police vans intensified in the form of an implicit, cautionary admonition to Hrudaya

Babu's night-friend that he should be in the hiding. A motor cycle passed by making a loud and ear-splitting noise, emitting volumes of greasy, blackish smoke into the air.

Perhaps this was the policemen's last round of patrolling. Some early morning birds twittered indiscriminately on some distant tree's branches, and then became astonishingly silent, as if being captivated by the early morning's mysterious and bewitching calmness. The moon had waned sufficiently in the sky that was patiently waiting for the sun to bloom like an effulgent lotus on its all-pervasive, empyrean firmament. The vaulted sky was slowly getting filled with rambling and diffused blotches of faint greyish patches prolonging like widening scars on its fecund body. In a few moments, those patches slowly turned red with the blooming sun's diffusive, nascent rays. In the meanwhile, the 'night-friend' had almost finished the second whiskey bottle.

On the main road, the thunderous sound of a moving truck was staggeringly audible.

Hrudaya Babu had finished the last peg. His eyes had gotten heavier with obtund and benumbing sleepiness. In a drowsy and drunken voice, he told: "If you come another time 'night friend' when my wife is not here, I will prepare bloody-merry cocktail for you in my own hands." But he could hear no response. He managed to force away his drowsiness and look round. The 'night-friend' had escaped by jumping over the gate. He had left on the bed Sujata's necklace and finger-ring.

Hrudaya Babu lifted them, squeezed them tightly in his scraggy, tremulous hand and suddenly became uncharacteristically serious and sentimental. For some time, he went on caressing the gold necklace with his hand and emitted a long, deep breath from his lungs, while two unruly teardrops rolled down across his beardy, frown-ridden cheek like two tiny, sparkling gemstones falling from his eyes. Perhaps they were the two sublunary remnants of his dead daughter Sujata's erstwhile earthly presence. His warm, temperate sigh infused some sultriness into the cold and freezing breeze of the wintry dawn. His two eyes were slowly getting closed...

The Flood's Companion

Govind Pattanaik! An old man! With genuflected posture, he sat on the ground and kept surveying the interminable profusion of circumambient flood-water around the little, ensconced and marooned isle. The water stretched unendingly beyond his blurring vision. Two rivers "Keluni" and "Baghuni" had joined together diabolically to generate this devastating flood that befell on the riverside-dwellers like destiny's abominable curse. There were only unfathomable greyish water, brimming bubbles and murderous whirlpools gurgling and frothing viciously around the isle; it created the ghastly monstrosity of imminent death that was set to devour the frightened souls on the isle with its fiery, cavernous mouth.

These two small rivers that usually lay emptied and waterless like two dead snakes throughout the whole year, had suddenly sprung into diabolic action to become a unified flinger of death and destruction on unprotected and endangered mankind. Because of a trench in Paika Bridge, they were filled with overflowing and voluminous masses of water thereby generating flood—a flood that was so fierce and annihilating that it could even cleave a snake that came its way into two halves. The submerged villages looked like distant isles that gleamed flickeringly with sunlight in the day and moonlight in the night. There lied at a distance the submerged Nachhipur village: only the bamboo forest's hairy, tousled top was sparingly visible, and also was unobtrusively visible the 'washed-away' and 'flood-plundered' top of the mango orchard.

Yes! Once the Mangarajpur dam had collapsed like this, all on a sudden with a loud and uproarious bang, generating a sweeping overflow of water that snowballed into an ugly and devastating flood. Govinda Babu pensively scrambled through the reservoir of old memories that kept haunting his troubled psyche like a pestilential ghost, even many years after the flood's actual occurrence. A few village folks including him went floating on a roof and were finally stuck on a little isle and were saved by the benevolent and protective almighty's assuaging providence. He was twelve or thirteen by that time. Now, carrying loads of experience in his mature and ripened mind, he is well-acquainted with the gravity of a flood-scenario. Today's younger generation nevertheless does not have much understanding of the cataclysmic power of flood. They harbour a false sense of security that there is a dam at the top which would never collapse and thus, there won't be any flood. All water shall be preserved in the reservoir.

But has this infinitesimally small creature called man ever conquered the indomitable might of water, wind and fire? Oh! The ripened corns were submerged in the ever-rising flood water. The mountain-like cornstalk was swept away in the flood. How could one stop it? It was heartrending to witness Nature's fury from such close quarters. It was all God's wish...

Phagu Rout was a school teacher. While leaving home for this small, 'protective-looking' isle, he had managed to bring with him this transistor radio that updated the flood-news every half-an-hour. One could wonder that they could exhibit more promptness in constructing dams rather than uproariously announcing flood news.

Govinda Pattanaik looked in another direction. "What shall I get from listening to that flood-news announcement? Will that mountainous mound of paddy come back? Will that gigantic pile of corn-stack come back?" He thought. Hari Dash rushed to listen to the flood-announcement: "The water level of the river is rising because of the release of eleven lakh cusecs of water from the reservoir. . ."

The transistor made a sudden, bizarre and jarring sound and stopped. "Hey! Why did you stop the transistor at the right time?" Hari Dash asked in an irritated and cacophonous voice. His nerves trembled with excitement. "When did I stop it? It's getting stopped at times due to sudden power failure." Phagu Rout said.

"O God!" Said Hari Dash. "The water level shall rise then." The waves of infernal terror rippling through Hari Dash's dazed and terrified eyes like the rising waves ravaging across the commoved surface of a convalescing sea were immensely visible. Phagu Rout intensified his fear by superimposing his frightening comments on Hari Dash's tormenting fearsomeness: "I think the water level shall rise even more. See the seething effervescence of water bubbles."

Govinda Pattanaik said: "Listen! It seems as if there is a cloudburst at the river's upper end. The thunderous uproar of the darkening clouds is audible from a distance. Hey look on! A dark cloud hangs like an ominous, giant vulture over your head." Hari Dash had heard from his infancy that if there is cloudburst at the river's upper end, then there will be a definite, devastating flood…

In a panicky gesture, Hari Dash threw a timorous glance at the accumulating flood water on all sides. He repented why did he imprudently come to this Talabani isle while his village folks went onto the canal bridge, instead, with their children and livestock? Presumably, it was a relatively safer place. But the next moment, he apprehended that the rising flood water might even submerge the canal bridge, engulf it like a water-monster. He conjectured that there was a fissure in that bridge; it could grow bigger and bigger thereby proliferating and widening the existing cracks in the bridge and then, the bridge might collapse, all on a sudden, crushed into a topsy-turvy mess of cracked soil and boulders inundated in the flood-water.

Was there any guarantee that such a thing won't happen? Now the Talabani isle might also be submerged under water for the water level was ominously rising, knowing no bounds, with water-hillocks piled on water-hillocks in enormous, hoarding masses. But people said that even the severest flood had not been able to submerge this isle, thanks to its unusual height from the sea-level. But, of course, it was all unsubstantiated hearsay. Initially, there was a small palm forest on the isle, embellishing its head like dishevelled, tousled lock of hair. But the farmers slowly started cutting the palm trees and there was not even a trace of the forest now. Now the isle lied completely bare, desiccated and forlorn apart from a lone, abandoned 'neem' tree standing at the top like an antique and derelict statue. Hari Dash started climbing onto the tree fearing the rising water level; he thought that the tree would be a safe haven for him due to its height. But he fell down.

Dasa Pradhan sat a little far away. He shouted: "Hey moron! Why are you climbing onto the tree? There are three cobras lying circled on the branches. I have seen them."

"O! Snake! Snake!" It looked as if Hari Dash's eyes bulged out in insidious terror.

Jayee Mohanty suffered from chronic osteoporosis in his waist. He could not stand straight. One would wonder how he climbed onto this isle with such a deplorable health condition guiding his way through the turbulently flowing streams. It was strange and inconceivable. The irrepressible jest for life had filled his body with unprecedented energy and vigour.

Hari Dash asked in his archetypal, apprehensive voice: "If the snakes come down from the tree and bite us?"

Dasa Pradhan kept staring at the flood water constantly and said: "In this flood, the enemies and friends are all alike. There were a black cobra and a boa taking shelter on the same floating roof on which we also had taken shelter." Hari Dash still could not be convinced and asked in a petrified voice: "If the rising water submerges this isle and if the snakes come down?"

Jayee Mohanty answered in a taunting voice: "Hey Hari Dash! You are a lone person. If you die, there is nobody behind you to even shed a single drop of tear on your derelict, abandoned corpse. Why are you so possessive and finicky about your sordid, solitary and companionless life?" There was a note of scathing sarcasm in his voice that penetrated into the depths of Hari Dash's slender bones like a cold, biting, wintry shiver. Hari Dash played harmonium in the village theatre group; he was its music teacher. He was so indulged in that group's musical activities that he couldn't find some convenient time for marriage and thus, remained single all through.

Hari Dash kept troubling everybody with his nagging,

irksome and unfounded fear. But Jayee Mohanty's taunt seriously disturbed his mind, like an oceanic convulsion. Who was after him, truly? He was almost forty. He couldn't get married till now. His age was also passing and he was getting older day by day. If he was swept away in the flood, the village folks won't even bother to search for his body. Then why should he bother so much for a life that had become uneventful, derelict and barren? But his desire for living was incredibly insistent and irrepressible. After all, man cannot relinquish his desire to live even in the midst of the acutest hazards and adversities.

Hari Dash went to a safe distance from the tree and tried to measure the water level. The radio announcement was right; the water shall rise. By this time, the level had already risen by a few inches more.

Dasa Pradhan said: "Today is the thirteenth day."

Hari Dash asked in a perturbed voice: "So what?"

"It's the full moon night and the moon's gravitational pull is in full swing. The billowing water-logging does not get cleared therefore. The swelling and surging tide doesn't allow the influx of river water into the sea. That means the flood water shall rise further." Explained Dasa Pradhan.

A helicopter was found flying very low while relentlessly rambling in the air, circuitously. Hari Dash lifted his hands and shouted: "Hey! Save us."

Phagu Rout said: "Hey! Hey! Have you gone mad? Shall the helicopter save us?"

Hari Dash said: "Then why it is flying in the air?"

Phagu Rout answered in a tone imbued with covetous sarcasm: "The sagacious ministers are greeting you from above, with benevolence and devotion. This is a clear and irrefutable testimony to their service to the people, to their never-ending humanitarian enterprise. The newspaper and the radio shall inundate them with boundless accolades and admirations."

Dasa Pradhan listened to all these while chewing a shrivelled piece of grass. He responded: "In earlier times, these ministers came on banana-trunk-made boats risking their lives."

Phagu Rout answered: "You don't understand. Today is the age of technology. Now the flood relief missions are carried out in a scientific manner; even though the flood is man-made, artificial. The time you speak of was different. Flood occurred when Lord Indra poured heavy rainfall on Earth, with divine wrath and vengeance against mankind's outrageous violations of 'dharma.' Now the engineers generate flood by opening the gates of the huge water-reservoirs."

Two more helicopters came rambling through the sky like two giant vultures with hitched, metallic wings.

Hari Dash lifted his hands into the air and shouted: "Hey Helicopters! Save us. Save us."

The food-packets thrown from the helicopters floated on the water surface, like rotten clusters of jasmines. Hari Dash asked: "What are these packets?"

Phagu Pradhan answered: "These are food packets. Have you not heard of food packets being distributed from helicopters during flood?"

Dasa Pradhan said: "They are distributing the food packets to the fishes. Will they ever reach the people caught up in the circumambient water-logging?"

Now they realized they have not eaten anything since yesterday. Their stomachs burnt in oppressive hunger that ran amok through their emptied stomachs like a congregated cluster of a hundred, squeaking mice. The scorching sun was hovering overhead like a revolving fireball emitting blazing rays of fire. Three or four paper-enwrapped food packets fell a few meters away from the Talabani isle. One of them fell within the diameters of Govinda Pattanaik's reach.

Somebody said: "Hey Pattanaik! Lift those packets before they are swept away in the turbulent stream." Pattanaik stretched his hand to catch hold of the packets. But for some strange and inexplicable reason, he drew them back allowing the food packets to drift away, in clumsy and disjointed clusters."

Dasa Pradhan asked in a stupefied voice: "What happened?" Alas! It would have been better if he caught hold of those packets. They had not eaten anything for three days. There was not a single morsel of food left in their stomachs.

Govind Pattanaik said: "I won't eat food thrown at us as if

thrown at beggars. In the last flood also, we had not eaten food for three consecutive days. After three days, a few people came on a banana-trunk-made boat and offered us parched rice and jaggery."

"Then was it not begged food?" Asked Phagu Pradhan in a bantering voice.

Govind Pattanaik answered: "No! No! They had offered us food with grace and honour. There was an ingrained sense of respect and dignity in that offer. It was not like throwing food from the sky and taking undue credit."

Phagu Pradhan stopped arguing and kept mum for he knew that it was fruitless in engaging in an argument with these abstruse, unyielding and rigid-minded older generation people. They had their own stupid and bizarre ways of understanding things and they could not be easily convinced about novel ideas and new ways of living. They were not ready to digest that their generation is outdated.

Jayee Mohanty shouted at somebody, in a shrilling voice: "Hey! You will drown. You will be swept with the current." Nata Kandi had entered deep into chest-high water to drag a few food packets floating away from him on undulating water. Holding three/four food packets in his hand, he came out.

Phagu Rout shouted in a tone of utter desperation: "Hey! Give one to me! Give one to me!" Nata threw one packet at him, unhesitatingly.

Jati Nanda was the revered village priest. His gluttonous mouth started watering looking at the food packets in a scenario where extreme hunger had made his stomach shrink without food. But how could he accept food from a barber? His sacred thread would be polluted and it would be a horrendous act of sacrilege for a sanctimonious priest like him whose consecrated body, mind and spirit were united in a hallowed, divine conjugation. He would have to undergo stringent purification rites, if he collected the food packet, unscrupulously, from a low-caste barber by transgressing the proscriptions of his 'dharma' and thereby, defiling its protected sanctity. Despite all his sacred inhibitions, he still could not control his curiosity and asked in a seemingly indifferent voice: "What food is there inside, boy?"

Nata Kandi opened one packet. There were two pieces of bread, some jaggery, two boiled potatoes, one candle light and a match box. Nata Kandi said to himself: "I wish they kept a few 'bidi's there."

Jati Nanda kept looking at the opened-up packet, surreptitiously, while trying to evade the hawk-eyed glare of the congregated and starving villagers. His stomach burnt in unbearable hunger. He saw Nata engulf the breads and jaggery at one go and looking at that scene, the abrupt and inextinguishable fire of hunger started burning more vigorously inside his starving belly. But he was helplessly caught in the whirlpool of a moral dilemma, an ethical imbroglio—how to collect food from an abominable low-caste wretch? But then, then suddenly an old saying from ancient scriptures flashed across the dark space of his mind like a sudden, evanescent meteor and readily resolved his moral dilemma. The saying was: "In utter need, there is no law" and its corollary was that everybody is the same when it comes to the question of hunger. With all his ethical dilemmas resolved thus, Jati Nanda said: "Hey Nata! Has the government thrown the packet only for you?" Jayee Mohanty is and old and ailing man. Why don't you give a packet to him?"

Nata was busy engulfing one boiled potato while peeling another's skin. He answered in an irritated voice: "When did I say no?" And then he started moving towards Jayee Mohanty to give him one packet."

Jayee Mohanty said: "Hey! Hey! Did you not understand Nata? Give that packet to Jati Nana[1]."

Jati Nanda almost confiscated that packet from Nata's hand and shouted vociferously such that everybody could listen: "In utter need, there is no law." Then he tore one packet with an expressive show of frenetic desperation and hurriedly gobbled one piece of bread. While chewing it with a crackling sound, he said: "Hey! Eating this bread is like chewing leather." Saying this, he bit his tongue apologetically. How could he utter such putrid words, being a devout Brahmin? Chewing leather...?

---

[1]   A Brahmin priest is called 'Nana' in colloquial language.

Phagu Rout got up from his place and ran berserk towards the isle's western side that had moved into deeper waters like an elongated peninsula.

Nata asked him: "Hey Phagu Babu! Why did you run there so frantically as if being entranced by a ghost?" Hari also came rushing in, fearing the unpropitious advent of a new danger.

Nata Kandi shouted while pointing his trembling finger at some hazy and unclear thing floating on water: "Mother Ganga! Mother Ganga!" Then everybody, keened by his voluble scream, looked in that direction curiously, including Dasa Pradhana. After casually surveying the scene, he sat down, with a condescending and disinterested disposition that was emphatically succinct on his face. Govind Pattanaik did not get up from his seat at all, and said: "A destitute lady comes floating on a roof."

In fact, they had also come floating on a roof like this once in another flood.

Nata Kandi started screaming again in another high-pitched voice: "Glory to Mother Ganga! Glory to Mother Ganga."

Nobody could conjecture from which flood-inundated village this blown-away roof came floating? One curly and twisted pumpkin creeper was still stuck curvaceously on its thatched top. A tiny and fresh flower had bloomed incandescently in that creeper; it kept tossing its flippant head to and fro in the whirly and rain-splattered moist wind, heedless of the utter devastation reigning all around. The lady sat on the roof like the sedentary effigy of an unknown goddess; she had dishevelled hair; her tell-tale dark and provocative eyes looked wide, stimulating and fluorescent; the eyeballs remained stubbornly insensate and unmoved and their adamantine immovability could be spotted from a distance. A faint and half-erased, rubicund vermilion mark still glimmered on her head, unwittingly, like the fractured and dispossessed fragment of a vanished star. The roof came nearer. Her face was burning bright with slanted sunrays, brushing across her rain-water-soaked, swollen face, tangentially.

Nata Kandi shouted again, this time with folded hands: "Glory to Mother Ganga! Glory to Mother Ganga."

Dasa Pradhan nevertheless spotted something worrying

and comminatory and shouted with sharp-toned note of concern: "Hey! The destitute lady is floating away. Drag that roof to the shore. If the roof is captured in the whirlwind, she will drown and die."

The roof was rapidly and unwaveringly drifting towards that murderous whirlwind. On it was sitting the destitute lady, with a grave and undeterred expression of stoic indifference dazzlingly implanted on her face, as a marker of cold and helpless acceptance of Nature's cruel and nonchalant vicissitude. She had turned speechless.

But if she was not Mother Ganga incarnate, would she not have shouted: 'Save me! Save me!"

Nobody dared to get into the drifting water full of swift and turbulently gyrating, murderous undercurrents. Somebody said: "Don't you all see there is not even a single blink in her eyes?"

Jati Nanda said: "Don't you all know the eyes of gods and goddesses never blink?"

Dasa Pradhan shouted: "Hey men! Get into the water. Get into the water and save the lady. She is floating away. I presume all her family members have been swept away by the flood's alacritous, pillaging, and drifty currents. She is perhaps the lone survivor. She has become deaf and dumb out of insurmountable grief and terror that have seized her after her interminable sense of loss. It happens like this with a traumatized flood-survivor."

By that time Hari Dash had entered into chest-deep water and was dragging that dilapidated roof ashore.

"Get down from that roof to safety, mother! Where is your village?" Dasa Pradhan asked the lady in a softened and fatherly, affectionate voice.

The destitute lady neither got down from the roof nor responded to his soothing words, while sitting mum and decidedly unresponsive towards the gratuitous bunch of gathered people looking at her with expressive airs of keenness and concern. She kept staring at them, dumbfounded, while being overawed by the brooding immensity of tranquillity and weirdness of this estranged isle.

Dasa Pradhan held the lady's hand softly in his and dragged

her onto the shore, to safety. The moment she landed on the isle, she burst into tears—streaming, unstoppable tears... There was no stopping to that piteous and heartrending wailing.

Dasa Pradhan said: "Leave her alone in that state. I am sure she has lost everybody of her family. Let her cry. Let her grievous emotions flow away through her therapeutic and relief-providing tears; let her be purged of her excruciatingly painful and agonizing emotions. Then only she will come back to her senses. Leave her alone."

The lady kept on bewailing ad nauseam and collapsed on the ground like a felled tree; her teeth were jabbed into each other; her soft hands had stiffened with the mulish and pertinacious tenacity of unbreakable metals; she had fainted. Hari Dash inserted his finger into her mouth and said: "Her teeth have been locked." And then he said worriedly: "What will happen now?"

Dasa Pradhana usually did not get provoked and irritated by anything due to his usually calm and imperturbable temperament. But Hari Dash had been constantly irritating everybody with his stupid and puerile questions. The former's patience came to end and he said in a fractious voice: "What else will happen? You are a bachelor. She has nobody with her now. So, now you will marry her and then, both will live together ever after. What else?"

Everybody started laughing boisterously.

The flood was receding. At places the sand patches were laid bare like the hard and glistening backs of tortoises slouching sluggishly across a waterless seashore's interminable stretches of sand. The massive, ripened stalks of corns were all swept away like lost, forlorn memories. The bamboo jungle of Nachhipur village started showing its drenched face from amidst the dull and insidious flood-ravaged vacuum created on the landscape by the receded waters. And also were seen from amidst the desultory masses of salvaged ruins, the broken relics of the village's dilapidated earthen houses... There was no trace of the Harizan[2] slum, though. There were no more food packets falling from the helicopters. The flood had subsided completely. The triumphant, cacophonic voices of ministers boasting and bolstering about their services done to humanity during the calamitous times of the flood were ceaselessly heard on Phagu Rout's transistor.

Nata Kandi said: "Let's all go back to our village. The flood water has almost receded. While going back, we might encounter occasional encumbrances formed by knee-deep or at best, waist-deep water-patches at places. But even in that case, why should we continue staying here, in this god-forsaken, marooned island, anymore with hungry stomachs, grieving hearts and tormented minds? The relief centre might have already opened in the village."

Nata Kandi was the first one to start walking, absentmindedly. Jati Nanda followed him, like his ubiquitous, uncomplaining, and obedient shadow. Dasa Pradhana and Govinda Pattanaik also started walking while muttering: "To spend time here on this swampy, abandoned and ghostly isle with hungry stomachs was perhaps cold-heartedly scribbled in our destiny, by God Almighty."

Phagu Rout said: "Hey Jayee uncle! Get up. I will hold you by your slacked arm in my hand arm so that you walk straight, without falling. Keep walking with me." Jayee Mohanty tried to get up from the ground with his bamboo crutch. Then he asked: "Where is Hari Dash?"

Hari Dash kept watching the destitute lady, unwaveringly, under the flood-ravaged, ramshackle, spooky and battered roof. She was getting back to her senses intermittently, looking around with wide, transfixed eyes as if her eyeballs would bulge out into the air and then, fainting while bewailing inconsolably.

Hari Dash said: "I cannot go leaving her alone, in this plight."

Jayee Mohanty said in a sardonic voice: "This Hari Dash has lived all alone throughout his life. Mother Ganga has arranged a bride for her."

While holding Phagu's hand, Jayee Mohanty started walking—unsteady and tottering— down the gravely, pebbly and winding path descending down the Talabani isle like a curvy rope, and mingling with the plain landscape lying stretched at the below like an unfurled, greenish carpet. A sarcastic smile hung on Jayee Mohanty's pale, blackish, gangrene-infested lips.

Jayee Mohanty's words ignited Hari Dash's hidden desire

---

[2] People belonging to the backward castes.

and his subdued prurience along with an abrupt influx of infectious desire running amok across his throbbing veins like a rapidly traversing wave. The lady lay flat on the ground, with her semi-paralysed, stiffened torso laid bare like an abandoned corpse; her half-closed eyes looked inebriated with an entrancing spell of grief; she occasionally muttered indistinct and discontinuous clusters of incoherent blabberings.

One of her breasts lied thoroughly uncovered. Hari Dash covered her breast with her own cloth which was lying unkempt and thoroughly bedraggled. He had gotten bored with his dull, apathetic and monotonous existence in Nachhipur village for so many years and that too, he was never an original inhabitant of that village. At times, a well-wisher asked: "Hari Dash! Will you never start a family?" He would mutter: "Who will give his daughter to a low-earning, forty-year-old like me?" But now it seemed as if Mother Ganga had arranged this bride for him, sympathetically, out of her own sweet volition for this lonesome, penurious devotee of hers. The lady had lost her family. The flood had swept them all away. Hari Dash also had nobody of his own.

The lady suddenly got up, screeched loudly and then sat straight on the ground, like a goddess's graffiti carved on granite stone.

The reddish light of the setting sun was scattered all over her face. Her eyes were still unblinking, and transfixed.

She asked: "Where am I? Where are they all? My Kuna and Muna?

Hari Dash was a little assured by the lady's return to her senses, unexpectedly though. He anticipated that by tomorrow morning, she would be alright. He said: "Don't worry. I am here with you. You came floating on a roof that was stuck to this Talabani isle."

The lady cried loudly again and fell flat on the ground.

It had been many times since then that she has gotten up, sat straight, perpendicular to the ground, with her legs stretched like two slender stems of a tree, shouted loudly and then, fainted. Throughout the whole night, the moonlight was flooded on her half-clothed body like a soothing, pain-relieving balm laced on her wounded torso filled with innumerable scars and abrasions— unspotted and invisible though.

Till now, Hari Dash had developed some kind of tender sympathy and fellow-feeling for the destitute lady due to her pathetic and deplorable plight caused by the devastating flood. But suddenly, this flooding deluge of moonlight splattered on her body reignited his buried, entombed passions that took the form of an extreme and manifest keenness and endearing infatuation on his part towards the destitute lady. Hari Dash kept looking at her half-revealed body with unblinking eyes and waited fortuitously till she came back to her senses again.

Nobody knew the exact time in the night. Two twittering birds reeled noisily in untraceable, circuitous trajectories in the night sky above the Talabani isle. In extreme exhaustion, Hari Dash had fallen asleep on the ground. He had anticipated that the lady would return to her senses in the morning.

When Hari got up from his sleep, the whole landscape was flooded with the morning's greyish sprinkle of light leaving the darkened and begrimed Earth awash with light and brightness. The moon had waned sufficiently in the sky leaving it spotless and pervasively greyish and pestilential. But where was that lady? The cloth-bundle that she clutched tightly in her hand when she came floating was lying out there—untouched, jumbled and abandoned. But where was she?

Hari Dash came outside. But the lady was nowhere to be found. He shouted: "Hey! Where are you?" He did not even know her name. There was a cryptic and comatose silence that prevailed all around, like a bewitching spirit engulfing every little tumult that could be heard. Like a moonstruck lunatic, Hari Dash kept sprinting along the whole landscape of the Talabani isle, from this side to that side. How could that lady disappear like this, wondrously, without leaving a trace? Or was it dream, a befuddling illusion? Or Nata Kandi was right? Was it Mother Ganga who had appeared in this destitute lady's mysterious, airy and apparitional form?

In the morning light, Hari Dash could spot her diminishing footsteps on the mud...

Adima and Satarupa

It was one of the nascent days of creation. In this prehistoric age, the Earth along with its ever-expansive world of primordial Nature along with its jungles, hills and landscapes had not yet been populated with human beings. The whole atmosphere was calm, serene and was bereft of the din and bustle of the clamorous human civilization. There were only two human beings on Earth: Adima and Satarupa—God's earliest and most exquisite creations. They quietly loitered in the forests like two noiseless phantoms, like two new marks on the whole creation's perdurable, timeless canvass.

Adima's job was to peregrinate randomly from forest to forest, from grove to grove and from hill to hill to procure food, by collecting fruits and hunting animals. He generated fire by rubbing one stone against another and illumined his caliginous vicinity with its fluorescent flames. An unfulfilled hunger and an endless craving for beauty were his inalienable companions. But there was also a strange sense of contentment in this unending quest for beauty.

Satarupa sat near a stream beneath the hill and remained submerged in the illusory and narcissistic appreciation of her own beauty, day and night. It was her pleasure and her delight—immense and unmitigated.

Like every day, she decorated her hair with the newly bloomed flowers and buds while looking at her reflection in a shimmering pond's crystal-clear water. A wild stag, enamoured by her exquisite beauty, licked her waist with a sense of utter ecstasy and boundless excitement. Satarupa's voluptuary body got charged-up with an inexplicable thrill and exhilaration. Her eyes craved for an unknown being yet to arrive; she felt his amorous and winsome presence near her in the touch of that wild stag's flirtatious tongue. But who was that mysterious and unknown 'being' that reigned supreme across the dreamy canvass of Satarupa's captivated mind? Or was it a mere illusion that she had fruitlessly harboured in the phantasmagoric landscape of her frantic and delirious imagination? Perhaps, the susurrant rustle of the leaves on the forest's un-trodden path had created the falsified impression of that esoteric 'being's mystifying and surreptitious approach. In her perturbed vision, Satarupa looked at the meandering trajectory of the path leading into the shadowy depths of the jungle.

As usual, Adima was returning home with a slaughtered stag placed on his shoulder. But today, his presence in her vicinity filled her inner being with insurmountable joy and profound contentment. The leaf-girdle that she was to drape around her waist dropped inadvertently from her hand. Her hungry eyes could not resist looking at Adima's bare, muscular body dazzling like pure, enamelled gold in the crimson light of the setting sun. But Adima disappeared into the fathomless forest throwing the dead animal onto the ground with a manifest expression of arrant disdain and condescension. A frantic rustle ran through the leaves of the forest with the uncatchable celerity of lightening. Satarupa left out a prolonged sigh of disappointment and got busy decorating her clusters of flexuous, silken hair.

These were the usual events in Adima and Satarupa's daily life. But it was a new dawn again...

The barren Earth waited anxiously for fresh creations after ages of accursed sterility. The enigmatic forest had become animated and restless in an ardent and irrepressible desire for creation. There was no soothing calmness in the raspy and blusterous streams of the hills; rather, there was a riotous bustle and virulence in their incessant and rambunctious flow. Perhaps it indicated their mad craving for creation. In the restive rustle of the undulating, farrago of leaves, there was an inexorable whim for regeneration. In the wetted, salivating tongues of the wild stags, there was an insatiate hunger for recreation.

Everything was so different now. The morning looked fresh; the evening looked unalike. A strange novelty emanated from the changing face of the creation, like an unprecedented parable scribbled on the mystifying pages of History.

In a voice that elicited an inexorable urgency, Satarupa shouted: "Adima! Adima!"

Her words were irretrievably lost in the insidious depths of the deep and impenetrable forest. Like every day, she could no more remain engrossed in the conceited beautification of her own body sitting on a spouting stream's outstretched shore. She disappeared into the forest while searching for Adima, hysterically.

After crossing many rivers, landscapes and hills, one day she spotted him in the un-trodden depths of the impervious forest. Adima was making a hunting weapon from a stone while sitting at the shadowy entrance of a tenebrous and ancient cave. While rubbing one stone against another, the taut and contracting muscles of his body looked clear and prominent and rippled like innumerable waves dancing sprucely on the infinitely stretched exterior of the sea. Satarupa silently watched the bursting nudity in Adima's body and while watching him, the rapidly spanning waves of her own desire merged with his illimitably undulating muscles. However, Adima did not care to look at Satarupa even once.

Adima always enjoyed preparing and collecting weapons for killing animals. He was a cold-blooded and rancorous killer. He never had a desire for creation.

Satarupa came and sat near Adima. To attract his fleeting attention, she plucked out a few blood-red 'palash' flowers from her hair and threw them offhandedly on the ground. While feigning incautiousness, she had keenly desired that Adima shall throw away his weapons and will fervidly decorate her hair picking up those fallen flowers.

But Adima did not look at her even once. To attract him, Satarupa caressed his muscles with her hand giving the former a delicate, enticing touch. Even now, Adima did not get attracted towards her.

Satarupa went away with a sullen and grumpy face.

Adima never understood the pain concealed in a woman's covetous and untended heart. So, Satarupa's facade of grumpiness went in vain. Thus, she came back and touched him again, amorously.

She felt that Adima's robust and stygian body was even harder and tougher than a mountainous rock's unyielding tenacity. It seemed as if he was the strongest progeny of Earth made of obdurate stones procured from the mountains. Satarupa wilfully poured her body onto Adima's to arouse his libido into a rabid and unbridled sensuous candour. Yet, his sinewy torso didn't soften; his nerves didn't vibrate in an aphrodisiac rhythm; his arms didn't surround her supple and curvaceous waist like a custodial barricade.

Adima's hunger was exclusively the primitive hunger of body; he had never been tormented by the hunger of the prehensile human heart. He won others only by force and virulence, but had never conflagrated himself in the incandescent fire of carnality, had never set himself ablaze with the desire for a beauteous maiden's fleshy and curvaceous body. He had always burnt others, but had never burnt himself in the fire of concupiscence.

Satarupa still did not lose hope. Her insatiate soul was filled with the unquenchable thirst for creation. Every tiny particle of her body vibrated in the desire for a sensuous, sybaritic union with her amorous partner. She kept waiting for Adima, with patience, with fortitude.

After some time, Adima felt hungry and sprinted into the forest like a predatory, wild animal maniacally in search for food. Satarupa followed him into the forest like his glutinous, elongated shadow.

After traversing a long distance, Adima suddenly came to a halt under a strange but beauteous tree. Satarupa also joined him there. They had no idea that the tree was filled with innumerable sweet and succulent fruits. Every fruit looked luscious and tempting from a distance and attracted even animals with its succouring allurement. Losing control over his burning gluttony, Adima jumped into the air and plucked a fruit from a lowered, heavily fruit-laden branch, and munched it with extreme contentment. It seemed as if a carnal and animalistic desire for creation was deeply embedded in every tissue of this succulent and delicious fruit. Adima had always relished the beauty concealed in destruction; but now, he for the first time encountered the same interred in creation. The fruit was filled with all earthly qualities—desire, sensuousness, pain. Like an injured and hungry, wild animal, Adima went on chewing the fruit, in the mad desperation of a predatory animal.

A strange, sweet but painful feeling captivated his senses with the immediacy of a lightening flashing across the murky canvas of an obfuscated sky. He saw Satarupa standing tantalizingly in his vicinity in the form of a fleshy and voluptuous virgin. He felt as if all the splendiferous beauty of the universe was crammed within her delicate, supple body that invited him for an amorous togetherness. Her flower-ridden hair was filled with the splendours of infinite, verdurous springs. Her inebriated eyes brimmed with an unquenchable desperation for union. In her quickening breaths, there was the odoriferous fragrance of Autumn.

Adima had seen Satarupa innumerable times before. But never before, did he feel so inevitably attracted towards her; never before did she look so new, so fresh and rejuvenated, so enticing and so sensually invigorating. Adima offered the half-eaten fruit to Satarupa by placing it near her mouth.

But Satarupa who had by now followed Adima like his inalienable shadow, now started running deep into the forest like a wounded deer hit by a hunter's arrow.

But where was she now?

In a moment the forest's lush, green body became brighter with the verdant greenness that Satarupa's wanton body emitted. Her flower-embedded wig ridiculed the forest's superabundant plenitude of flowers.

Adima started following Satarupa shouting her name relentlessly.

But where was Satarupa?

His shout for Satarupa reverberated through the distant hills, their ravines, valleys and forests, like multiplying echoes emanating from the voluptuous Earth's rapacious heart. Yet he could not get her.

Many days later...

Finally Adima spotted Satarupa. Like every day, she was busy decorating her hair looking at her reflection on a hilly stream meandering like a swift virgin evanescing through the hill's dark and preternatural caverns, while chuckling frolicsomely. Its little, swift waves washed Satarupa's denuded feet with an immense profusion of paradisiacal delight.

Listening to Adima's restless shout, Satarupa looked at him once and then, continued decorating her hair heedless of his unfeigned desperation. Adima was now irresistibly excited at the sight of her beautiful, semi-nude body flickering before him like the unexplored reservoir of a bewitching mystery. He felt like lifting her in his arms and running irretrievably into the crepuscular depths of the tenebrous forest; it seemed as if Satarupa had hypnotized him with her indecipherable, hypnotic allure and had captivated his soul like a fiendish sorcerer. She had immolated him completely with her desire.

Adima called in a seemingly terrified voice "Satarupa! Satarupa!"

But Satarupa did not look back at him, even once.

Then Adima came again. He held many delicious fruits and dazzling flowers in his hands, as precious gifts for his beloved Satarupa. The latter, after taking a fresh and sanctimonious bath in the stream, had opened up an incomprehensibly illusory world before Adima—a world that had ensnared him with its inconceivably bewitching dexterity. Placing the fruits and flowers below her feet, Adima called: "Satarupa! Satarupa!"

Satarupa felt like looking at Adima lifting both her downcast eyes. But nobody knew what happened today. Adima's body, glowing with the resplendence of a thousand splendid suns, had blinded her eyes. She could not look at him.

Adima emitted a long breath of utter chagrin and went back...

He came again the next day holding a soft, glittering, deer-skin-made dress as a novel gift for Satarupa.

Adima told: "Come Satarupa! Come to me! Throw away your leafy and lacklustre attire; I shall cover your body with this soft and beautiful dress made of deerskin.

Satarupa could not say anything substantial and fittingly reciprocative in response. Her voice had turned mute and inaudible. Looking at Adima, she desperately wanted to cover her thoroughly denuded and uncovered body with her criss-crossed arms, which nevertheless were found cumbersomely inadequate. She covered her breasts in her hands and in a way, protected herself from the penetrative glances of Adima's lascivious eyes.

Adima's carefully brought gift lied scattered on the ground. He again slowly disappeared into the forest like the last expansive breath of the dying spring.

The next day he came again, this time with a pearl-made garland as a gift for Satarupa.

Losing all control this time, Adima put the garland around her neck.

He was mesmerized by the touch of Satarupa's soft, pallid torso. It was soft, yet bereft of her usual briskness and virulence.

It seemed as if Satarupa had turned into a lifeless, stone effigy. She did not reciprocate to Adima's inviting touch.

Adima was again going back emitting a deep, mercurial breath. But this time Satarupa felt like holding him back from behind.

By the time she could respond, Adima had already disappeared into the mazy and intricate depths of the forest.

He came again the next day. But this time there was no gift in his hand. He came as a lone, destitute being, bereft of the ardent virulence of an avaricious lover. He only had the tormented feelings of her heart as a gift for Satarupa.

Satarupa looked at Adima lifting both her eyes. Adima didn't know what strange intimacy lay concealed in that cold, haggard and incapacitated look of hers. But his soft inner 'being' hidden under his stony muscles, started trembling like the fluttering limbs of an arrow-hit animal.

Adima could not understand anything. What a revivifying sensation ran surreptitiously through every tendon of his throbbing muscles! What excruciating pain moved through his shivering veins!

Was it a sensation indicating the desire for a bestial union?

Two drops of tears flew through his stony cheeks like two serpentine hilly streams flowing along a rocky, rugged terrain. He was flabbergasted. What a pleasurable feeling it was! What pain! What desire to lose oneself in this outrageous expressiveness of bestiality!

Of course, his successors termed this ingenuous feeling as 'love.' But to Adima, this aberrant feeling seemed more blissful and sacramental than the forest's sumptuous greenery and the amaranthine bluishness of the infinitely spread-out sky.

Adima was preparing to leave again. But this time Satarupa stopped him from behind and dragged him onto her breasts.

From both her eyes also flew two streams of unstoppable tears.

Amrapalli

I

That day, the conference hall of the Lichhabbi[1]-union in Baisali did not have space for even a piece of grain. It was jam-packed. Everybody, starting from the commoners, the royal personages, the intellectuals, and the businessmen, had assembled there to witness the assembly's proceedings and to listen to the union's ultimate judgement on Amrapalli[2].

In such gatherings on other occasions, one hardly found the simultaneous presence of all the members of the commoners' union inside the gigantic hall's vast and expansive inner space; but today, everybody had occupied their respective positions inside the hall with utmost excitement and enthusiasm; they waited for the instructions of the convener to start the proceedings.

The convener got up from his seat to pacify the noisy and bustling audience and said: "Please listen to me, respected members. There is no need to maintain quorum today. Because, as far as I can see, almost all the members of the Licchabbi community are present here, in this grave and auspicious occasion. Therefore, I request the chief whip to commence the proceedings." At the instructions of the convener, the chief whip Deepankara stood up from his seat and said while addressing the audience,

---

[1]   It's a clan that lived in the ancient Indian kingdom of Magadha.
[2]   Amrapalli was a beautiful lady of Magadha during 500 BC (roughly) who had to turn into a public whore under certain circumstances as described in the story. She ultimately became Lord Buddha's disciple.

emphatically: "Esteemed convener and all the respected members of the committee. May I kindly have your attention, please? Before listening to the committee's final judgement on Amrapalli, please listen to her life story narrated by her foster-father, the gardener Asitabarna."

Asitabarna stood up from amidst the assemblage of the commoners, looked at the amassed crowd with a hawk-eyed, revolving stare, paid soulful obeisance to them with folded hands and said: "Dear commoners! I am the caretaker of the mango orchard at the outskirts of Baisali[3]. Today, I recapitulate my life's most preposterous yet memorable event that occurred sixteen years ago, inside this mango orchard, at Baisali's outskirts, filled with the dense foliage of pullulating trees and with the flooding moonlight of the radiant moon that had soared high up into the sky like a golden-winged eagle. It was not yet morning. The collective, restless twitters of the morning- birds woke me up from bed, very early, when the reddish sun was just beginning to bloom like a lone, incandescent lotus in the eastern sky. The wind had gotten heavier with the fragrance of the proliferating mango buds inside the orchard, and their intoxicating smell initiated me into the slow, savoury advent of the blooming dawn. I suddenly heard the relentless cry of a new-born baby lying abandoned in the chequered gloom of a secluded corner inside the orchard. I had been childless all my life and had always longed for one. I wondered whether it was a crude game of destiny or God almighty's providence lying strewn before me as a rare and prodigious gift. I remember that day vividly even today, despite the fact that the passing years have impaired my memory and all the reminiscences of my past life have irretrievably slipped into the realms of oblivion. That day, some destitute lady had abandoned this beautiful baby below a mango tree; even her umbilical cord was not severed. Without contemplating anything, I lifted her onto my lap. I did not care whether she was the blasphemous child of some obnoxious whore or even a curse to mankind; I just accepted her as my own

---

[3]   An ancient Indian city.

child. Sixteen years later, today she is your Amrapalli—Baisali's ill-fated beauty."

At the end of Asitabarna's narration, chief-whip Deepankara left his seat, got up and said: "That Amrapalli is today Baisali's terror, a living curse, an anathema. I wish she died the death of a vermin and let us live in peace."

Convener Ganadhara asked: "But where is Amrapalli?"

Suddenly, the symphonic music of her anklet was heard outside the palace, with its rhythmic echoes and reverberations filling the empty air with its enthralling, jingling cadence. Unclear, seething voices rose from the assembled crowd: "Here comes Amrapalli. Here comes Amrapalli."

Amrapalli was blue-bodied; her soft and spongy feet were dyed with reddish hue in a design that looked like the scattered congregation of pomegranate seeds; her thin waist was covered with a golden string that elongated up to her thighs like a sonorously downflowing cascade; her arms and breasts were embellished with golden jewelleries; below her curved eyelids were placed two undulating, drunken, deer-eyes; they looked like the string of Madana's[4] bent, curvaceous bow.

Deepankara said: "The republic of Baisali lies endangered only for this contemptible beauty, Amrapalli. States like Bideha, Malla and Kalama are all madly hankering after this accursed beauty. Are you cognizant of the fact dear commoners that the enormous wealth of this poor gardener's daughter can even ridicule Baisali's huge and unmatchable royal exchequer? If our secret information is correct, the Magadha king Bimbisara, being irresistibly enamoured by this virgin's enthralling beauty, contemplates abducting her into his palace. Everybody of us would be aware that it's not entirely impossible for an incorrigible lecher like Bimbisara whose anecdotes of habitual debauchery is a universally known phenomenon. If Bimbisara continues with his salacious advances towards Amrapalli, then a military conflict between Baisali and Magadha is inevitable for Baisali would definitely resist such mean, salacious and indecorous advances

---

4   Madana is the God of love and lust in Indian mythology.

by this despicable usurper. But of course, its dire consequences are also not hidden from us. For how long Baisali's small military establishment can sustain itself in front of the unsurpassable might of the gigantic Magadha army? So, it is my humble and sincere supplication to all of you that as per the customs of the land, let Amrapalli be declared a public-courtesan before all. For the finalization of this proposal, I solicit a referendum."

Like a deer being afraid of the hunter, Amrapalli looked at the assembled citizens with her eyes overflowing with heartrending effluxes of pity and terror. At this point in time, another member Silabhadra got up and said: "This voting is not required at all as this proposal is unanimously acceptable to all, without an iota of doubt; I believe even Amrapalli won't oppose this proposal that has, in fact, been mooted by the revered commoners for safeguarding the safety and sovereignty of Baisali."

Thus, the proposal for a formal voting was readily repudiated by the assembled commoners, unanimously. Amrapalli's compulsive conversion to a public-courtesan was authenticated and ratified by the assembled members through mass clapping and raucous howling.

The convener Ganadhara got up at this point in time and said: "Esteemed members of the union. With your kind permission, I declare that Amrapalli henceforth becomes a designated public-courtesan. Her beauty is her crime."

II

During the time, which is represented in this narration, this was the custom in states ruled by the communities like Shakya, Koliya, Bideha, Maurya, Buli, Kalama and Bhaga etc. The virgin whose beauty generated insurmountable conflicts between different kingdoms, territories and communities was ultimately forced to become a public-courtesan, or rather, a public whore such that she remained available for civic consumption and thus, unwarranted conflicts between kingdoms and territories could be readily avoided. As per the prevalent custom of the day, Amrapalli was declared a public-whore in Baisali, in the mentioned commoner's assembly. But it must not be forgotten that she was still a remarkable and intellectually enriched lady of the Buddhist times and the stories and anecdotes eliciting sparks of her intellectual competence are legion. In *Theri Gatha*[5], there is present a touching and tearful autobiographical anecdote written by Amrapalli herself delineating the pitiful plight of a public courtesan during her time; she was treated as no more than an object of the common populace's sexual gratification. It recounts the poignant story of how that day, Amrapalli had sacrificed all the pleasures of her life for Baisali—the pleasures of her womanhood, the delight of blissful motherhood, the hopes and aspirations of a joyous, exuberant life—everything.

But it must also be acknowledged that the public whores during the mentioned era were not simply consumable sex objects for men; rather, they also possessed the highest levels of competency in literature, music, dance and many other forms of art and craft. In addition, they were unimaginably wealthy in a way that their affluence could ridicule that of the kings and other royal personages of eminence. In the Buddhist text *Binayapittaka*, we can peruse the biographical details of Kashi's illustrious whore "Ardhakashi" whose one night's income could equal one day's revenue contributed by the citizens for the royal exchequer. But since she could not get customers at such a high price, she had halved her price. Thus, from that day onwards, she became known as "Ardhakashi."

III

Amrapalli's gaudy and sumptuous bedroom in her palace in Baisali! She lay half-conscious on her heavily cushioned cot, after giving birth to a gorgeous and attractive baby boy. Her maidservant Sirima stood beside her with a new-born baby in her lap, and intended to say something to Amrapalli.

Sirima called: "Elder sister."

Amrapalli opened her tired eyes with great diffidence and said in a harsh, repudiating and contemptuous voice: "Why do

---

[5] An ancient Buddhist text containing autobiographical poems by women poets.

you stand there Sirima? Go and throw that baby on the roadside. It will be morning after a while."

Sirima told: "What a beautiful, princely baby! It looks exactly like King Bimbisara. I don't feel like throwing him away, elder sister."

Amrapalli's tormented motherhood raised its head again, and her voice softened for a moment being overpowered by the natural benignity of compassionate motherhood.

Sirima told in a softened voice: "Take the child onto your lap, elder sister. Take the child onto your lap."

But Amrapalli's mood altered suddenly and she screamed like a trampled serpent: "No! No! That's a blasphemous child. He is an incarceration for me. An abominable curse of this life! Go and throw him out right now, Sirima. I would have kept her if she was a girl child. But it's a baby boy. Go and throw him right away. I don't want to listen to your futile arguments anymore, Sirima."

The baby started crying inconsolably on Sirima's lap. Amrapalli started shouting: "Press the cloth in his mouth Sirima. Let him be finished. Why do you stand here? Go."

Sirima pressed the baby closer to her breast and left, with a sullen and grumpy face. Amrapalli felt like taking revenge on herself, on an abandoned and neglected life that she was living in the midst of the brooding despair and gloominess of a begrimed and feculent whore's life.

But why were these streaming tears flooding across her schmaltzy eyes? She could not have been so weak, so vulnerable, so emotional, so mawkishly sentimental. After all, she was a courtesan, a public whore.

IV

By an incredible stroke of destiny, that day's abandoned child later on went on to become a famous Ayurvedic[6] doctor— Gautama Buddha's disciple, Jeebaka. But there is of course no

---

[6] An ancient medical practice in India involving the treatment of diseases through herbs and other arborescent materials as medicines.

chronological record in History that recounts, with credible evidence, the growth and nourishment of this abandoned, nameless, parentless and destitute child of Baisali into a famous doctor in the hands of a childless man.

V

Many years later...

Amrapalli's whorehouse remains pathetically empty and people-less. Her spring-tree like body that was once suffused with unrestricted pullulation of wealthy and ensnared lechers, has now become pale, haggard, desiccated and abandoned. They have left for younger Amrapallis. She is now sick with an incurable disease; her emaciated body is fully paralyzed, and incapacitated. In her dancing feet, there prevails the dull and sombre inertness of rocks; in her once flashy and shimmering golden body, there is the dark and terrorizing reign of death. A cataract has invaded her deer-eyes, like a pervasive, irremediable mildew. Padmabati is now Baisali's new public whore. Wherever one goes, he hears only praises, eulogies and adorations for Padmabati, as if there was no Amrapalli ever in that region.

VI

On the sick bed, lied Amrapalli's filthy and diseased body, like a lifeless and abandoned object. Jeebaka sat beside her and rubbed some balm on her eyelids. Amrapalli shouted like a mad woman in distress and screamed in an anguished and grief-stricken voice: "Give me some poison Jeebaka. I don't need this life. I know Jeebaka my lost youth won't come back; my lost vision shall not return. Your efforts are futile, Jeebaka. Your efforts are all futile."

Jeebaka rubbed his hand delicately on her forehead and said in a cosy and consolatory voice: "Be quite mother. Rest assured. I shall bring back your youth; I shall bring back your health."

Jeebaka was blessed with a magically alleviating touch in his hands. His words never turned out to be false and inconsequential. Harbouring an unbounded confidence in his immaculate, curative prowess as a physician, Amrapalli had completely surrendered herself to him. "Oh! What solace! What calmness! There is wonder in his hands. What affection do I feel when he utters the word 'mother'!" Amrapalli said to herself and wanted to look at him even with her blinded eyes. But for her, everything was hazy and indistinct, like blinding layers of thick and condensed fog. She remembered the day when she held the baby in her breasts and felt the unbounded and eruptive joys of contented motherhood. She felt the same joy today with the divine touch of Jeebaka's calm, soothing hands on her progressively decaying, diseased body.

Amrapalli asked; "Who are you Jeebaka?"

Jeebaka answered: "I am a beggar, mother. I am a beggar. Without being perturbed, you take a nap, mother. I assure you will be completely cured, very soon."

Amrapalli was not yet amply satisfied and convinced with Jeebaka's reassuring and confidence-providing words and answered: "But this is not your true recognition Jeebaka. Tell me who you are."

Jeebaka emitted a rhapsodic flicker of smile on his face and answered: "The identity of a beggar is that of a beggar, mother. He does not have a father, a mother, a wife, a son, a daughter and a world of his own. He is only a beggar. He is liberated from all binding and obligatory worldly entanglements."

Amrapalli responded in an affectionate voice: "Sit beside me for a moment, Jeebaka. Oh! My eyes are paining severely. Rub your calm, soothing hand on my shrivelled, desiccated forehead once more, Jeebaka."

Jeebaka obliged like an obedient child. A deep satisfaction and a calm repose filled Amrapalli's inside being like Lord Buddha's holy, palliative and consolatory blessings.

Jeebaka, while rubbing his hand on her forehead, told: "This is the ultimate truth of this world, mother."

Amrapalli asked: "What truth, Jeebaka?"

Jeebaka answered: "This disease, this old age, this infirmity, this fret, this suffering! Youth is transient and evaporative mother."

Amrapalli asked: "Then what?"

Jeebaka answered: "This world is an illusion, a tantalizing mirage, mother. Desire is the cause of all grief and suffering in this mundane, sublunary world fraught with fret, disease, decay and afflictions. Renouncement of the world is the only panacea, the only pathway towards ultimate liberation. That is why the prince Sakya Singh[7] is a monk today, a happy and contented denouncer of the world.

Amrapalli asked: "Who is that Sakya Singh?"

Jeebaka said: "I shall tell you his story today."

******

Amrapalli was slowly recovering through Jeebaka's recuperative treatment and care. Her vision had not yet completely returned; yet, she could see everything, though a little hazily and unclearly.

That day when she saw Jeebaka for the first time, she felt as if her heart was extirpated with a hunter's acuminous arrows. This Jeebaka—a beggar! If her abandoned child lived, he would have looked exactly like this Jeebaka, this angelic Jeebaka, this godly alleviator of the pain and suffering of the sick and the diseased. The same appearance! The same vast and sprawling forehead! The same twinkling, glittery pair of eyes! The same sword-like nose!

No! No! Why should Jeebaka be this filthy Amrapalli's bastard child? He is a god, a reincarnation of divinity, a godly saviour of tormented mankind. Oh! What sense of un-fulfilment! What hunger! What desire! What desperation to clutch him in her lap! Two streams of glitzy and glittering tears flowed form Amrapalli's eyes, while glistening flashily in the crimson light of the setting sun.

Jeebaka asked: "Are you crying mother?"

"No! No! Why do you call me mother? Call me Amrapalli; call me a whore; call me by whatever foul and feculent name you like." Amrapalli answered. But could she not be called a mother? If her own son sat beside her sick bed, if he saw tears in her eyes,

---

[7] The prince of the kingdom of Kapilabastu who later on renounced the world and became Lord Buddha.

he would have certainly asked: "Are you crying mother?" But here was Jeebaka who had sacrificed everything for the 'Sangha[8],' who had relinquished every dull, banal and telluric pleasure of this earthly life for the sake of salvation.

Jeebaka asked again: "Are you crying mother?"

Amrapalli wiped off her tear with her saree and said: "No Jeebaka! There is slight pain in my eyes."

Jeebaka assured her with his calm and comforting words: "You don't worry, mother. The pain shall subside."

Amrapalli responded: "Yes Jeebaka! You had promised me that day to tell me the story of Sakya Singh. Tell me the story now."

Jeebaka started telling Amrapalli the story of Sakya Singh.

VII

Gautama Buddha shall come to Baisali.

The news had spread in every nook and corner of the city, like internecine, wildfire spreading unstoppably through a jungle.

The Lichhabbis were busy welcoming the Lord as per their customs and conventions. Baisali's men and women were ecstatic and desperate to see him, to get his blessings.

In the meantime, Jeebaka had completely cured Amrapalli and restored her into her normal health and wellbeing. With Jeebaka's godly, curative treatment, she was restored to her youth and splendour, just like a moon being freed from the demonic Rahu's[9] bewitching and fatal clutch. But a deep and pensive thought, a sordid realization of something baleful and augural had descended upon her clear, luminescent eyes like the pervasive shades of pithy, dark clouds; some unspeakable grief had swindled away their wealthy lustre.

Jeebaka told: "Do you know mother? Lord Buddha is coming to Baisali."

Amrapalli said; "But how useful is that news to me, Jeebaka? I am a filthy whore. My body is an object for sale. For public

---

8   The Buddhist religious community.
9   It is, according to Hindu mythology, a devilish power that engulfs the moon in the dark moon night.

consumption. Am I capable enough to have a look at the holy Buddha?"

Jeebaka answered with a curious smile: "Who is not a whore mother? Your body might be an object for sale. Not your soul! But those who have made their bodies and souls cheap, sellable objects, are indeed more abject and despicable than you. These Lichhabbis of Baisali! Have they not sold their conscience in the name of 'dharma'?"

In both the eyes of Amrapalli, danced the lucent, dazzling flames of scorching summer.

Today, King Bimbisara shall arrive in Baisali. The messenger from Magadha had brought this news.

Today Buddha will come to Baisali.

There was a huge and unprecedented commotion in Amrapalli's palace. Every corner was decorated with attractive and odoriferous clusters of flowers whose captivating and winsome aroma had spread through all directions like the unctuous and seductive odour emanated from the sedate and voluptuous body of Earth. Amrapalli told Sirima: "Today, the guest will come, Sirima—the long-awaited guest."

The full-moon evening of spring! Amrapalli's orchard at Baisali's outskirts was filled with the enthralling fragrance of innumerable, mango buds. After many days, Baisali had decorated herself in the beautiful and sensuous attire of an ornate and bedecked bride awaiting her man on a gaudy, flower-embedded, nuptial bed. Chandra helped Amrapalli wear the anklets over her ankle, the golden thread around her dark, slender waist, and the golden bracelets around her smooth, dusky arms. Sirima sprayed her hair with intoxicatingly aromatic perfumes. Holding a dazzling mirror in her hand, Amrapalli laced a lustrous and effulgent tinge of vermillion on her forehead.

Everywhere there was a magnificent commotion; today will come king Bimbisara.

Like a joyous, exuberant river dancing elatedly on the rocky pavements of a hill, Amrapalli's heart throbbed with an abundance of joy and exhilaration. For today will come the Buddha, her long-awaited guest.

Amrapalli told in an excited voice: "Shyama, Chhanda and Sirima! Don't delay any more, friends. The full-moon-night's moon blooms in the sky like a golden lotus, emerging from the darkened silt of Earth. Look at its crimson petals. Look how they spread and diffuse into the dense, inebriated evening air steeping every earthly thing in its crimson colouration." There was frenzy and excitement in her voice.

Sirima decorated Amrapalli's wig with florid and glitzy clusters of dazzling Ashoka[10] flowers.

The highway roiled with the deafening noise of the amassed, bustling and rambunctious crowd. Amrapalli frantically ran towards the window and looked at the outside world booming with noisy, blusterous festivity. An attendant rushed in and said: "Madam! King Bimbisara waits for you in the luxury room."

Lord Buddha is coming to Baisali. Baisali's citizens revelled unrestrictedly with mirthful joy and exhilaration.

Amrapalli came rushing in from the window and told, elatedly: "Hey! Here comes the guest, Sirima! Let this luxury items be left here."

Amrapalli sprinted outside like a mad woman. From her dishevelled strips of hair flying in the air like thin clusters of disjointed clouds hovering listlessly across the bluish firmament of a trenchant sky, fell many Ashoka flowers, intermittently on the ground, filling the desiccated air with their bewitching and fragrant aroma.

The poet's violin stopped. King Bimbisara rubbed his eyes with surprise and disgust.

Baisali's royal whores were left speechless.

The Buddha lifted his deific, shimmering hand into the air to bless Amrapalli, in her ostentatious and glitzy Luxury chamber. With her gorgeous and dandified attire looking conspicuously pale and lacklustre before the Buddha's glowing face sparkling with divine splendour and luminosity, Amrapalli prostrated on his feet like a felled tree.

---

[10] A beautiful flower that blooms on the plant of *Saraca asoca* in the Indian subcontinent.

The disciples sang in a chorus:
"Buddham saranam gacchami,
Dhammam saranam gacchami
Sangham saranam gacchami"
(I take shelter in Lord Buddha,
I take shelter in the holy religion,
I take shelter in the holy community)."

The Salvation

I

The morning chorus of Grudhrakuta Vihara's[1] disciples sounded like the humming of a hundred flies.

"Om namah samasta buddhanang apratihata sasanam."

(We bow before the undefeatable intellectuals.)

On the thick, stolid branch of a tree inside the mango orchard, an impatient cuckoo sang a shrilling mating song for its partner." Nilotpala kept listening to it uninterruptedly.

Nilotpala was a salvation-seeking Buddhist disciple. He had wilfully relinquished all earthly bondings—love, lust, sensuality, desire... How could he then have appreciated the cuckoo's sensuous, sublunary mating song?

He said: "Hey stupid bird! I have no interest in your sensual mating song. Yet, I know that it is regarded as the best symphony in the world of music. What a terrible irony! Your song is the salvation, an unfathomable emptiness where all beings dissolve. Yet from within this emptiness, does emerge a brimming completeness—the completeness of all beings, all existences.

The cuckoo's song penetrated through the inmost recesses of the mango-orchard, and kept on echoing like the reverberations of an undying desire.

For a moment, Nilotpala forgot his divine chantings, and

---

[1]   Here it refers to a Buddhist monastery.

started listening to the cuckoo's sensual song. Willy-nilly, he was getting attracted.

He looked through the window at the trees' branches in Grudhrakuta-Vihara's mango-orchard; they looked to him like a nude woman's sharp, fleshy limbs spread out against the vast expanses of a golden sky.

Nilotpala concentrated on chanting his divine songs. If he chanted these mantras one lakh and eight times, he would have received divine blessings from Lord Buddha.

As a dedicated disciple, he should have refrained from imagining a woman's nude limbs in the mango tree's branches in a spring morning. He was a salvation-seeker and as a principle, must have stayed away from such impious, worldly imaginings. A contingent of Buddhist disciples marched towards his chamber while chanting spiritual mantras and listening to them from their mouths was for Nilotpala another step closer to salvation. The usual duty of these salvation-seeking Buddhist disciples was to light candles before the statues of Buddhist gods and goddesses like Abalokiteswara, Pragyanparamita, Amoghasiddhi, Tara, Akhyoba, Lochana etc. placed in the ancient caves, and then to roam from chamber to chamber in Grudhrakuta-Vihara spreading Lord Buddha's divine messages all around.

Nilotpala looked like getting up from a dream. And then he chanted: "Om namah samasta buddhanang apratihata sasanam."

(We bow before the undefeatable intellectuals.)

The disciples met Nilotpala in his room, lighted the candles with ghee and left. The sanctified ambience got holier and heavier with the smell of burnt ghee and wick.

But where was the lady whose anklet's symphony Nilotpala was desperately waiting to hear? Where was Swetaparna's beautiful daughter-in-law?
"Ah Madhubrata!" Thought Nilotpala for a moment.

In that ignited moment in a tranquil night, her memory shook Nilotpala's whole being like a sharp sting of pain.

Forgetting his chantings, he shouted inadvertently: "Madhubrata! Madhubrata!"

Last time, Madhubrata did not come to the sacred ceremony.

A few days before that, Nilotpala's friend Bajrabahu had met her in her abode when he roamed from house to house for begging. That day Madhubrata had offered alms to him in her own soft, delicate hands. But as a principle, a disciple once after collecting alms from one household, was not supposed to visit the same for a stipulated period of time. So, Bajrabahu did not have the liberty to revisit Madhubrata's in the immediate future.

Nilotpala shouted: "Ah! Madhubrata!"

Madhubrata's pair of tormented eyes flashed for a moment in his memory like two pieces of sparkling diamonds and then, vanished. In Nilotpala's frenzied imagination, they again looked like two half-bloomed lotuses in a still-water pond and then delicately sparkled like two glittering, globular dew-drops dangling from the delicate blades of soft grass.

"Om namah samasta buddhanang..." Chanted Nilotpala.

Another Cuckoo's sensuous mating song was heard from within the distant mango orchard. It silenced his chantings.

Nilotpala felt like asking his guru Acharya[2] Santideva about what really is eternal? This cuckoo's desperate mating song? Or the chantings of divine mantras?

For a moment, he felt that every argument, every divine chanting would become silenced one day; but the bird's sensuous mating song would remain eternal.

"Then why should one relinquish every earthly pleasure and enjoyment and indulge in self-abnegation and then, venture into unforeseen realms of salvation?" Nilotpala asked himself.

There were two red-granite statues placed inside an ancient groove in Nilotpala's chamber. The statues were of Abalokiteswara and Pragyanparamita, both in meditation, but in tight, passionate embrace. Some disciple had placed at their feet a few clusters of the dazzlingly reddish 'Ashokamanjari[3]' flowers. Pragyanparamita's soft, delicate breasts were pressed closely against Abalokiteswara's wide, open chest. On both their faces brimmed a deep and profound sense of heavenly contentment.

---

[2]   An ancient name for a Guru.

[3]   A red-coloured flower that blooms in the Indian subcontinent. Its botanical name is Saraca Asoka.

The night had become silent. The inmates of the 'Vihara,' after wholeheartedly confessing their sins and moral blunders before Acharya Santideva, returned to their chambers happy and contented, being disburdened of their previous sins and fallibilities. They slept peacefully in their chambers.

But Acharya Santideva was still meditating on a dear-skin-mat outside his chamber situated in his building's third storey in Grudhrakuta Vihara. In the night flooded with the deep and unrestricted profusion of moonlight, he looked like a darkish, immovable stone effigy. In the vastly spreading light of the moon, the shades of the orchard's mango trees looked like dark and gloomy strips and patches scattered all over the Earth. A tattler bird screamed restlessly in the moon-blanched air as if to awaken the night that slept like an innocent virgin on the Earth's cushioned bed.

At Nilotpala's untimely call, Santideva opened his eyes, and stared into the former's dark and perturbed eyes that looked gloomier than the night's enshrouding darkness. Acharya Santideva knew so far that Nilotpala was one amongst the best disciples in the whole 'Vihara' in terms of observing sacredness, self-abnegation, and spiritual perseverance. He could not imagine that even Nilotpala might fall prey to such ignoble, worldly fallibility. He therefore asked: "Hey Nilotpala! What makes you come to me in the middle of the night?"

Nilotpala could not provide an abrupt answer and kept quiet for some time. His voice vibrated with an honest confession.

He finally admitted in an unambiguous voice: "Acharya! I have fallen in love with disciple Swetaparna's daughter-in-law Madhubrata. She was married to the former's son Nalinakshya who, after their first night, went on a trading-voyage across the sea with a few fellow-voyagers. It was a few years ago and from that day onwards he is never seen again. Some of Pataliputra's[4] traders who have returned home from their voyages across the beyond-the-sea islands say that he has been killed by sea-pirates. Some others say that he has started a new life with an unknown

---

[4]   The capital city of the ancient city of Magadha.

lady in a foreign island. Swetaparna, after prolonged and fortuitous waiting for his son's return, has finally accepted that he is dead and hence, has completed all essential, religious death-rites for his son. Everybody has reconciled to destiny's cruel verdict that Nalinakshya is dead. Yet, Madhubrata is living with a futile expectation that he will come back one day — a hope that is alive like the un-extinguished wick of a candle."

******

A soft autumn afternoon! As per the usual practice, Nilotpala after finishing his meal in disciple Swetaparna's house, was preparing to leave before dusk. Madhubrata accosted him through her chamber's window: "Nilotpala!" (Nilotpala felt the soft, pleasing touch of her blushful voice along with her bracelet and anklets' sweet symphony deep within his soul. It was beautiful and enchanting like the cuckoo's tender, mellifluous singing in the mango orchard, like the soothing twitter of the tattler bird in the tranquil, moonlit sky.)

Before Nilotpala, appeared the blue-gown-clad, the flower-embedded, the slim-figured, the dusky-complexioned, and the beautiful Madhubrata. Her dye-ridden feet were full of a musical symphony. Her slim, supple figure was lascivious, enticing. But her eyes that looked like inverted lotus leaves were filled with the stoic indifference of a shadowy lake. Nilotpala was mesmerized.

Nothing but the incessant hooting of pigeon busy lovemaking in the sty was audible in that languorous afternoon.

With the touch of Madhubrata's deep breath on his skin, Nilotpala got back to his senses. He looked into the enormous depths of her eyes. Her face was almost washed by a few tear-drops fallen from her lotus-eyes. Her softened lips vibrated with a question.

Nilotpala asked with a sympathetic voice: "What would you ask me, dear?"

Madhubrata stretched her left palm towards Nilotpala and asked in a blushful voice: "Can you look at my palm and prognosticate whether my husband whom I had said adieu with the setting sun over River Ganga will return or not? He has left me after our first night and has never returned."

Nilotpala held Madhubrata's left palm in his hands like a hypnotized man. Palm-telling was indeed a prohibited art for the Buddhist disciples and thus, it was not possible for him to answer to her questions. Yet, he kept on holding her soft, spongy left palm in his hands in that mesmeric afternoon. It seemed as if his hungry nerves and tendons were rejuvenated with a new life, a new sensation. Nilotpala felt like getting lost in a trance. It seemed as if his whole existence was getting dissolved in a fathomless vacuum. He felt that the profound emptiness that he had been searching for years through deep meditations and had not yet gotten was achieved in this captivating moment, in Madhubrata's supple touch in this dusky, pigeon-infested afternoon. His whole being was thoroughly shaken up.

"This is the great, inexplicable emptiness in which everything dissolves—body and soul, flesh and appearance, everything. This touch is the greatest pleasure through which the body transforms into the bodiless. This is salvation." Thought Nilotpala! The profound happiness that was visible on Abalokiteswara and Pragyanparamita's faces was also felt by him in that bewitching moment.

His deep, warm breath was as if burning Madhubrata's soft, delicate palm. She slowly dragged it back from Nilotpala's hands and hid it in her saree[5]. Her eyes slowly closed down beneath her descending brows.

Nilotpala got back to his senses, but Madhubrata had left by now. His wakeful trance was gradually coming to an end in the midst of the pigeons' relentless hooting inside the sty.

****

Santideva sat in his meditational posture as usual. The tattler bird's frenzied shouting had made everybody realize the moonlit night's immense tranquillity and loneliness.

Nilotpala told Santideva: "Hey guru! The day Madhubrata touched me, I have lost all control over myself. My body's desire has gotten reignited and has undermined my pursuit for divinity. But O Guru! In that touch of the moment I have realized salvation,

---

[5]   A typical long-clothed attire that Indian women wear.

that eternal emptiness which we all are aspiring for. Is this realization false, Gurudeva[6]?"

Santideva was sitting like a meditating Buddha. Nilotpala's questions reverberated in his ears like the tattler bird's sharp cry in that tranquilized night-sky.

He answered: "Nilotpala! Tathagata[7] has discovered the panacea for suffering. The cycle is like this: "Thirst born from the desire for beauty leads to pain and suffering. So, to get rid of suffering, you need to conquer your thirst, and to do that you have to relinquish your desire. Now relinquishing desire paves the way for salvation—liberation from the cycle of birth and death."

Explaining this, Santideva got back to his meditation. Nilotpala stood like an immovable shadow against the wall. The restless tatter bird climbed higher up into the sky and then, descended into the mango groove's shades like an insatiate, thirsty soul and then, kept on traversing across the night's excited nerves like an unstoppable whim, an irrepressible desire. It climbed up again and then, circled the moonlit sky weaving shifting, twisted patterns in its vast, sprawling vacuum.

The moonlight spread across the sky like the unfastened attire of the denuded Urvashi[8]. Nilotpala was lost in the hypnotic allure of that incandescent flood of light. Tathagata had said: "Desire for beauty is the cause of grief; it is a hindrance to salvation." But this beauty gave Nilotpala pleasure, not pain— this moonlit night, Madhubrata, the softness of her palm! They were beautiful, enchanting, enticing. In that touch, Nilotpala felt the infinite pleasures of salvation. But of course, this pleasurable moment was transient; it came, embraced him and disappeared.

Nilotpala's desire for more of Madhubrata's proximity was getting ignited like a volcanic eruption. It was burning the cool, tranquil moonlight into ashes.

Santideva told him in a cold and calculated voice: "Son! It's late in the night. Now you go and sleep. But as a step towards the

---

6   A respectable term for teacher.
7   Another name for Lord Buddha.
8   A heavenly nymph in Indian mythology known for her beauty.

attainment of salvation, you have to spend three weeks inside the crematorium from tomorrow onwards."

Nilotpala came back from the 'Vihara' into his chamber. The candle below Abalokiteswara and Pragyanparamita's statues had gotten extinguished long before. A thin ray of moonlight had scattered almost imperceptibly on the chamber's stone-floor. The tattler bird's restless shout in the night sky kept him waking till late in the night. He was mesmerized by the smell of the mango buds.

*****

That day while returning to his place, Tathagata was taking rest with his disciples in a Sal-forest at the outskirts of the Malla[9] community's village. It was springtime and its joyous atmosphere had spread through the whole forest like his heavenly blessings. From within the forest's enormous depths, a cuckoo's desperate song was calling the former to wake up from its sleep. The song created an upheaval along the Sal-forest's green foliage while the ceaseless humming of the jungle-bees added to the noise.

At this point, the thought of women disturbed disciple Ananda's mind who asked Tathagata: "God! What should be the relation between women and the disciples?"

Tathagata answered: "Every disciple's duty is to stay away from women."

Ananda asked: "Hey God! But what if some beautiful lady comes your way some time?" Tathagata answered: "Then you have to control yourself by subduing the fickleness of your senses."

Ananda asked again: "Then what will be relationship between the disciples and women?"

Tathagata answered: "The disciples must refrain from verbal interactions with them."

Ananda asked again: "If a lady starts interacting with a disciple?"

Tathagata answered: "Then quietly go away from her with a downcast head."

*****

---

9   An ancient Buddhist community.

The last rays of the moon hovering high up in the distant horizon came through the open door of Madhubrata's chamber and fell on her tormented pair of eyes that were slowly closing down. The still night's plaintive wind got ignited with her long breaths.

Nilotpala got up from his stone-bed and closed his chamber's doors.

II

A long, sprawling crematorium lied stretched on the shade-less, shrub-less top of the Grudhrakuta Mountain. On that ground, Nilotpala desperately searched for something in the midst of the congregated human bones, skeletons, skulls and the tattered dresses, as if the mystery of the whole creation laid concealed in that mess. Without shave, his head was full of long hairs whereas his chin was covered with a huge beard. His sparkling, bright face looked pale and wrinkled and his shrunk skin looked hard and lifeless like dry flesh. His ochre-coloured dress looked banal, without any noticeable grandeur or sophistication. He wore an abandoned dress as an undergarment. His eyes were sunken deep into their sockets and looked blood-red in colour.

Guru Santideva's orders were clear and unambiguous: "As long as Nilotpala does not conquer his desire and his senses, he can never be a complete Buddhist disciple." Nilotpala had till now not been able to do that. His desire for beauty and the thirst for the body still persisted in his subconscious. That is why on the orders of Acharya Santideva and as a norm for the salvation-seekers, he was sent to this crematorium to practice self-abnegation through meditation.

All these salvation-seeking individuals had to go through the same process of self-abnegation in the crematorium so that they could realize the transience of this body of flesh and bones which will ultimately perish in the crematory fire. So, this momentary desire for physical beauty is nothing but a futile illusion. Nothing shall remain permanently; this beautiful body shall also perish one day. This realization was of utmost importance for someone who was on the pursuit of salvation. A triumph over beauty, desire and grief is the pathway to salvation and Nilotpala was to master this craft.

On the burnt valley of the noon, the cool shade of the mountain-range came down like a soothing balm. At the crematorium's outer edge, a herd of vultures came flying from the dead branches of a lightening-burnt tree sniffing a corpse nearby. The vultures descended at a distance and started rubbing their beaks against the ground. Nilotpala thought that some corpse was lying out there and hence, ran towards it. The vultures still remained unperturbed and were heedless of his menacing approach. Nilotpala lifted a stone and threw at them so as to drive them away from the body.

Someone had placed a corpse beneath the cover of a stone. Nilotpala lifted the stone in both hands so as to have a look.

A grief-stricken father had placed his toddler's tender body on a carefully prepared bed of leaves such that it would not be damaged by the rough touch of the pebbly and rugged soil. He had placed near the body a colourful toy... the baby's playmate. Oh! This child looked like a soft, delicate flower fallen from its stem. It was heartrending for Nilotpala to look at his face.

Nilotpala never had any sense of attachment with children previously; neither did he have any innate feeling for them. But this time he wanted to lift the tender baby in his arms. But then he stepped back at the sight of a poisonous snake. A blue colour had spread through the baby's skin. His tender lips had turned black.

Nilotpala cried with a grief-stricken voice: "O God! I cannot bear this sight. The baby has turned into a green corpse. It's unbearable God! It's unbearable."

Nilotpala shouted again: "This body! This body! It's beautiful and powerful for only a few days. Then... Then... A day comes when it becomes food for dogs and jackals and vultures, then for worms and germs... Then... Then...

Nilotpala lifted his hands into the vast expanses of the sky and shouted: "Then... Then..."

His words hit the mountains around the empty ravine and echoed: "Then... Then..."

Then he said: "It's then a congregation of scattered bones, of pounded bones... Nothing else."

In his frenzied imagination, Nilotpala saw Tathagata telling Ananda in that Sal-jungle: "These colourless bones are the ultimate consequences of your desire for beauty, your hunger for flesh..."

Nilotpala started shouting like a mad man: "Bones... Bones..."

Then he lifted his muscular arms into the air and shouted at himself: "Nilotpala! These are not your muscular arms. These are a pair of dry, desiccated bones. Nilotpala! You yourself are a colourless, worm-infested bone."

But then why would a piece of bone seek salvation?

Nilotpala looked at the sky and shouted: "Can you tell the sky what is the need for salvation for this piece of bone? This piece of bone does not have another birth! It won't come back; it does not have a desire for flesh; it does not have either discontent or grief... It's only a piece of bone. Only a piece of bone!"

Then it's all salvation... Great happiness. Liberation from the cycle of birth and death!"

The gloomy shade of the mountain-covered ravine condensed into the tranquillity of the surrounding. A deep commotion from the Earth's tormented soul painted the horizon with a sprawling, reddish hue.

On the other side of the crematorium, another group of corpse-carriers were returning across the dusk's murky and crimson light.

The task of practicing self-abnegation in the crematorium entrusted to Nilotpala by Santideva had been completed. Nilotpala had now understood the mystery behind birth and death and thus, the futility of this earthly life, of this body with its meaningless beauty and sensual appeal. The beauty and sensuality of a woman's body could no more entrap him; they could no more arouse in him the primitive demon of desire. Today, Nilotpala was liberated from the incarcerations of the thirst for body, liberated like an arrow unleashed from a bow. Now he could get back into his ensconced meditation-chamber of 'Grudhrakuta Vihara' with a happy and contented disposition.

The spring had lost most of its beauty and grandeur.

From its burnt-out bed, summer was rising vigorously with its ruthless and burning blood-red eyes.

Today Acharya Santideva would coronate Nilotpala with the accolade of being a complete Buddhist disciple. After that, the latter would be known as Kalyanamitra[10] Acharya Nilotpala.

He no more had to sit beside a corpse and watch the pantomime of life disappearing into the flames of death. Today all his perseverance had come to an end. Today was the most auspicious occasion of his life. Nilotpala suddenly remembered: "Today is a full moon night."

By this time, a new corpse had entered into the crematorium. Nilotpala could not resist the temptation of throwing a cursory glance at it. And then like a wild animal sniffing the prey, he moved towards the corpse with slow and measured steps.

In a secluded corner of the thorny, shrub-infested crematorium, the corpse-carriers had kept a blue-attire-clad body beneath the cover of a few stones. Nilotpala lifted these stones in both his hands.

It was a woman's corpse lying on the ground. Except her face, her whole body was covered with one blue attire. Oh! A woman! A woman! A burning flame! In the frozen darkness of the crematorium, it was lying abandoned—cold and stiffened. Nilotpala rubbed his sunken eyes and looked at the body inside the graveyard's shaded groove.

Gosh! It was Swetaparna's daughter-in-law Madhubrata.

The same Madhubrata whose beauty had enamoured him and had thwarted his salvation-seeking endeavour! Nilotpala had come to this crematorium to stay away from her vicinity such that she no more remained a hindrance to his spiritual pursuit. But she had followed him even after her death. For Nilotpala, to confront her was like digging an old wound. To get rid of his attraction towards her, Nilotpala had roamed across the crematorium like a ghost, scrambling through corpses after

---

[10]   A title that authenticates someone as a successful Buddhist disciple.

corpses, to unravel the mystery behind the vicious and inexplicable cycle of birth and death. But today, his tormented past had come back to haunt him, to confront him; it had stuck to him like an unbreakable shadow.

In a moment, all his perseverance, all his spiritual endeavours disappeared like the gentle breeze of spring.

The same blue-attire-clad, slim-figured Madhubrata! It seemed as if she was looking at him, with her lotus-eyes, with her dilated eyebrows. Her reddish lips were open and inviting him for a union. There was a blushful expression on her face.

Like a hungry, wild animal, Nilotpala took off the dresses from her body in both his hands. He held her nude, lifeless body in tight embrace while feeling its sensuous touch on his own skin. They were becoming one; they were merging into each other, just like Abalokiteswara and Pragyanparamita in those statues in his chamber. Nilotpala started kissing every part of her body vigorously like a lunatic. He showered her denuded body with his kisses. He was going mad. He was losing himself in her.

Nilotpala had no idea that Acharya Santideva was already standing behind him, neither was he interested to know that. He was lost in his mad passions.   Acharya Santideva shouted in an angry voice: "Nilotpala! Nilotpala!"

Nilotpala did not answer. He just held Madhubrata's nude, lifeless body in tight embrace on his chest, kissing her frantically across her neck and face.

Santideva shouted again; "What the hell are you doing Nilotpala? What are you doing, you moron, you senseless fellow? What are you doing?"

Nilotpala neither looked at Santideva nor was he disturbed by his presence.

He was lost in true salvation.

Over the mountain range, the luxuriant moon soared high up into the night sky like a wingless eagle. Nilotpala lifted Madhubrata onto his shoulder and started running deliriously into the darkness of the grooves.

Santideva was helplessly shouting from behind; "Nilotpala! Nilotpala!"

In the empty ravines of the mountain range, Santideva's shout was getting echoed and ricocheted towards him like a crude and biting sarcasm from the mountains.

Holding the nude and dead Madhubrata over his shoulder, Nilotpala was progressively getting lost in the darkness of the grooves.

Srikrishna's Last Laugh

That day it seemed as if the sun had stopped his chariot for a moment to witness the concluding scene of *Mahabharata* in Indraprastha.

After the end of *Mahabharata*, Kurukhsetra's abandoned battlefield was filled with the dispersed debris of many ornamented chariots and with the mutilated bodies of millions of Kaurava soldiers scattered all around. Their distressed wives led by late Duryodhana's wife Bhanumati frantically ran through the field looking for their loved ones from amongst the gigantic and petrifying mounds of bodies. Their heartrending screams submerged and obfuscated the loathsome and terrifying shouts of bloodthirsty dogs, jackals and the vultures.

Death had engulfed every little commotion in Kurukshetra. Every sound including that of the horses and the tuskers had become tranquilized under its pervasive and marauding spell. The battlefield was infested with swarming army of wild dogs and jackals whereas above in the stultifying sky, reeled like dark shades the flesh-loving kites in large flocks.

Dhrutarastra's palace in Indraprastha had turned disquieted and people-less. At times Sanjaya and Bidura were found to be loitering helter-skelter inside the tranquil room with plaintive moods. The slow sound of their footsteps made the overall climate of the palace grave, gloomy and pestilential. Dhrutarastra's pitiful sighs and Gandhari's heartrending cries were getting heavier.

Dhrutarastra was blind from birth. He had lost all his

hundred sons, his friends and lieutenants including Karna, Drona, Bhurisraba etc. in Kurukhsetra's battlefield. His buoyant aspirations to see them for the last time ricocheted from the four walls of his room and were sealed in its comatose, cadaverous silence, like incarcerated birds in a cage. But Gandhari thought of throwing away her eye-cover and seeing her son's bodies for the first and the last time; but her proscriptive and irrevocable vow during her marriage to Dhrutarastra, as a devoted wife, made it impossible for her. As a sanctified and ceremonious wife, she could not have crossed over the ethical circumscriptions laid down by herself. But if she had not vowed that day, today she would have easily thrown away her eye-covers to see those bodies.

Gandhari was the mother of one hundred sons— Duryodhana, Duhsasana, Durjaya, Duranta, Durgama, Durtara, Durbalaka... ; she was the glory of Somabansa[1]. The sons who slept only on the gorgeous, comfortable cushions on their cots, now slept on their murky deathbeds in Kurukhsetra's muddy, pestiferous battlefield.

The egregious rampage of dogs, jackals and kites on their bodies created a ghastly scene all around.

Gandhari emitted a sharp cry of pain when she heard the intimidating sound of a flock of kites swooping feverishly on the abandoned bodies.

She lifted both her arms into the air and cried: "Bidura, Sanjaya..."

Her pitiful cry echoed for some time inside the hall and then was engulfed by the ghostly silence of the pathetically depopulated Kaurava palace.

*****

Blind Dhrutarastra lifted his two arms into the air with a futile display of inconsequential vainglory and boasted before Bidura: "Don't forget Bidura! Even today I have the power to smash the Kaurava-killers—these Pandavas—to dust, in my two arms."

Dhrutarastra shouted like a lion sitting on the dazzling but disenfranchised Kaurava throne. The muscles on his wrinkled

---

[1] The glorious clan into which Gandhari and the Kauravas belonged.

face stiffened obdurately. His eyes sparkled like a dead volcano sprung to life.

Bidura told in a cool and composed voice: "Your Excellency, great king! All the Dhrutarastras are eternally blind. The power and vainglory of the throne has perennially eclipsed and obfuscated their vision. Eyes are not the only vision, king. Where was your vision when the Kauravas wanted to treacherously finish off the Pandavas in the lac- house? Where was your vision when the five sons of Draupadi were slaughtered, bestially, in sleep? Where was your vision when Draupadi was denuded and puckishly humiliated in the fully occupied Kaurava palace before everybody? Where was your vision when Duryodhana boasted, while vaingloriously thumping his chest, before Srikrishna's convoy that he would not give the Pandavas even a pinch of soil without war? If you had been jurisprudent and righteous as a king during those conflicted times, today you would not have confronted such unwelcome and dire consequences, my king. That is why I keep reiterating that it is not just you, but it is all the Dhrutarastras who are perennially blinded."

Dhrutarastra answered; "But I had never thought, even in my wildest fancy, that the great warriors like Bhisma, Karna and Drona etc. will be so easily defeated and decimated by this impoverished and destitute bunch of Pandavas."

Bidura answered: "That is why I keep telling that all the Dhrutarastras are perennially blinded. The demands for justice by the exploited, however weak and vulnerable they may be, can never be trampled and suppressed by your oceanic and deleterious Kaurava army. History shall always derogate and ridicule many Indraprasthas, many Hastinapuras and many Barunabantas for their blatant and meaningless exhibition of ineffectual vainglory. The great King! The peace and sovereignty of 'Bharata[2]' shall be achieved not through the callous humiliation of the destitute, rather through uplifting them with a sagacious display of kindness and fellow-feeling."

Listening to Bidura's sermonic admonitions, Dhrutarastra

---

[2]   The ancient name of India.

started shouting in a way as if the sky would tumble on Earth with an uproarious bang. Lambasting Bidura with a grave and thunderous voice, Dhrutarastra said: "Bidura! You are the slave of the Kauravas. You have grown up on the food and kindness provided to you by your so-called callous and vainglorious Kauravas. Today, when they are in great distress, you are giving them the appropriate gift with your unkind and hurtful words. There is not even a single word of comfort and solace in your voice for the Kauravas."

Bidura responded with an unperturbed voice: "Great King! Truth, however bitter, tough and unpleasant it may be, has to be confronted one day."

Dhrutarastra shouted again: "But for a small and insignificant territory, the whole Kaurava race will be demolished. Do you agree to it, Bidura?" How would I forget Bidura? The flagrant, lighted candles of the Somabansa are getting extinguished one by one. Like my own blindness, the future of my race looks bleak, inconsequential and dismal."

Bidura responded in a cool and unruffled voice; "The great king! Accept this destiny as a consequence of your relentless and grievous wrongdoings. You will get peace. You have destroyed your own race by turning blind eyes to their prolonged and persistent injustices and misdeeds. Pandavas are only a small, negligible race. Don't harm them any more out of your injudicious anger and vengeance."

During that time, the grieving Gandhari came rushing in like a mad woman with her eyes blindfolded and said: "Great king! One day I had wilfully put these covers on my eyes as an inviolable vow, as a token of sympathy and honour for your accursed blindness. Liberate me from my oath today great king. I am the mother of your one hundred sons. I have never seen them in my eyes when they were alive. Let me see them today when they are dead. Let my grieving eyes get some conciliation and solace."

Gandhari wanted to tear off her eye-cover with a feeling of an unstoppable and undeletable urgency to see her dead sons' bodies, splayed right in her front. In the process, she inadvertently scratched her face with her fingernails and started bleeding copiously from the wound. The blood oozing from her injured face made her look terribly ugly, mephitic and gruesome.

Gandhari shrieked again in an awfully broken voice: "Great king! I have always remained blindfolded because of you despite having my healthy vision intact. Today, take off my eye-covers for once great king and let me see my dead sons."

Listening to Gandhari's requests, Dhrutarastra's face became pale and lacklustre like a piece of dark, febrile cloud. Gandhari did not know (But Dhrutarastra knew) that below that superfluous cover, there were not just her dormant eyes, but were two giant, hibernating volcanoes. Once she opened them, even Dhrutarastra would burn to a shapeless pile of ashes within a few moments.

Bidura tried to comfort Gandhari and told: "Try to control your grief great lady. Who tells you do not have sons anymore? Under the protection of the Pandava king Yudhisthira, your son Durdasa is still alive." Moreover, the five Pandavas love and adore you like their own mother."

Gandhari started shouting again: "I know great king! This eye-cover shall never come out. Right from the beginning till the end, Gandhari's life will only be about noxious darkness and irremediable grief and nothing else."

Gandhari had come floating towards Dhrutarastra like a dry, desiccated, windblown leaf; and went back like the same blown away in a passing, twirling whirlwind.

*****

The festooned chariot was ready to glide towards a preordained destination, carrying the war-triumphant Dharmaraja Yudhisthira on its cushioned recliner. In the nick of time, Srikrishna approached him from an opposite direction and asked: "On the eve of your propitious coronation as Hastinapura's celebrated and illustrious king, where are you going alone Dharmaraja[3]?

Yudhisthira said; "Mother Gandhari has summoned me. I am going to meet her."

---

[3]   Yudhisthira was famously called 'Dharmaraja' for being the protector of 'dharma' or righteousness.

Srikrishna responded peevishly: "I have also not met mother Gandhari for quite some time now. Then let's go together. I shall drive your chariot."

Yudhisthira was taken aback by Srikrishna's abrupt and unsolicited propositions and asked: "What is this new mystery, Mayadhara[4]?"

Srikrishna sprung onto the charioteer's seat and responded in his archetypal, alchemistic voice: "Do you forget Dharmaraja I am the one who had led this once blood-stained chariot to victory through Mahabharata's sanguinary battlefront. Are you doubting me, Yudhisthira?"

Embarrassed and shame-faced, Yudhisthira kept mum.

Srikrishna had always remained a mysterious character like this.

*****

Gandhari roamed with Sanjaya through the mass grave of Kurukshetra's battlefront while madly scrambling for her one hundred sons from amongst the massive and horrendous pile of blood-stained bodies. In the diminishing lights of the dusk, Sanjaya led her through the ravenous crowd of dogs, jackals and kites into the midst of these bodies scattered all around like dried and crumpled leaves strewn putridly over a storm-ravaged landscape.

Sanjaya told: "Great lady! Look how the legendary Bhisma lies out there on the soil in the deepest slumber of his life. Look at the hermetic, calm repose on his face." Gandhari said: "I know Sanjaya! He has relinquished his life in his own volition. Otherwise the Pandavas were nothing before his world-beating might."

Sanjaya said: "And here lies the war-hero Somadatta, smashed under a chariot-wheel and there lies the great Bhurishraba wounded to death by the mad tusker's internecine tusks. Great lady! Here lies the war-hero Karna, barged by the arrows of archer Arjuna. On the split and fractured crown on his head is stuck the last ray of the setting sun, like the deific blessing of the father on his son's head. With that ray's sparkling luminosity,

---

4   Krishna was called 'Mayadhara' for being an expert in the art of creating 'maya' or illusion.

Karna's face still glows with the resplendence of a hundred blooming lotuses in a sun-bathed, shimmering pond."

Gandhari held Karna's body in her breasts in a tight, passionate embrace and said in a choked voice: "Come boy! You have been deprived of a mother's affection all your life— you, the greatest Pandava. Come to me. Let me embrace you. You, the protector of Duryodhana's arrogance! I cannot see you lying here in this wretched condition on this muddy and abandoned battlefield. But O almighty! O omnipotent! O creator! Is there no retribution for those who have defied the Khsatriya[5] principles and killed Karna through treachery?"

After moving some distance, Sanjaya told: "Great lady! Here lies Duhsasana deflated on the soil, his thighs smashed by Bhima's gigantic mace. It was Bhima's vow to avenge his obscene behaviour towards Draupadi's denuded thighs in the crammed Kaurava court. His pearl-decorated necklace still dazzles on his wide chest, like the sparkle of lightening across the jumble of blue clouds. Let's go great lady! This is the eternal game of life and death. Everybody is entitled to his deeds."

A vexatious outburst of a sharp cry of pain filled Gandhari's voice and she told: "Remove my eye-cover once Sanjaya. This is the son whom I have never seen in my life. At least let me see his body and pacify my eyes."

A little away from Gandhari, Srikrishna curtailed the speed of his chariot. Yudhisthira asked in a fretful voice: "Why did you decelerate the chariot's speed, Narayana[6]?"

Srikrishna answered with a gentle but carousing smile: "We should not go with the arrogance of victory to someone who suffers from unbearable pain and agony. In addition, Gandhari is like your mother."

Yudhisthira got down from the chariot like a wrongdoer and said: "You are absolutely right Narayana. I should go to grief-stricken mother Gandhari on bare foot."

---

5 It refers to the race of warriors. They are expected to fight the battles on the basis of certain heroic principles, not through deception.
6 Another name for Srikrishna.

Yudhisthira was nonchalantly walking towards Gandhari sitting and bewailing rambunctiously near Duryodhana's slain body when Srikrishna hastily pulled him back by one arm and said: "Do you know Yudhisthira why Gandhari has summoned you?"

Yudhisthira said: No! I do not know that."

Srikrishna smiled gently again and said: "Gandhari wants you to remove her eye-cover so that she can see the bodies of her sons from amongst the pile in Kurukshetra's crematory ground."

Yudhisthira told: "Is it a very difficult thing to do?" I shall tear off her eye-cover this moment."

Srikrishna smiled astutely and told: "But Yudhisthira! How do you forget that the mother of one hundred sons Gandhari is today sonless because of you Pandavas?" In her comprehension, the whole of the Kaurava race has been demolished because of your lofty aspirations for the throne."

Yudhisthira told in a helpless voice: "I don't know whether she knows it or not; but you know it all great God."

Srikrishna answered: "After you remove Gandhari's eye-cover, she would see her son Duryodhana's body first and then will she not be filled with a feeling of anger and vengeance instead of that of love and compassion?"

Yudhisthira asked in a stupefied voice: "That is true Krishna. But when mother Gandhari has called me to do the job, what should I do?"

Srikrishna told: "All the hundred sons of Gandhari might have perished; but her son Durdasa is still alive. Gandhari's anger can be pacified when she sees her son Durdasa."

Gandhari could hear Yudhisthira's voice from a distance when the former conversed with Srikrishna and she asked Sanjaya: "Sanjaya! Is this not Yudhisthira's voice that I hear?"

Sanjaya said: "Srikrishna and all the Pandava brothers have arrived to pay obeisance to you, mother."

Exalted, Gandhari lifted two of her arms in the air to embrace Yudhisthira and told: "Come, Yudhisthira, come! The living embodiment of compassion, the Pandava leader! Today you are also the Kaurava leader. I am the sinner; I have received the consequences of my misdeeds in the past. Please remove my opaque eye-cover once, son. I have never seen my hundred sons when they were alive; let me see them in their death for the last time and let me pacify my craving eyes."

Listening to Gandhari's pitiful words, Yudhisthira was going to remove her eye-cover; but Srikrishna stopped him from behind by holding one of his arms. Then he turned towards Gandhari's only surviving son Durdasa and said: "Durdasa! You go and remove your mother's eye-cover. The mother who has lost almost all her sons will at least get some consolation to see her only surviving son."

There was a mysterious smile in Srikrishna's lips.

Yudhisthira told Durdasa: "Do what says Srikrishna."

Durdasa wilfully obliged Yudhisthira's orders and expeditiously removed Gandhari's eye-cover.

The moment it was removed, the conflagrant flames of infuriation and vengeance flung outside from within the dark and infernal pits of her eyes like an impetuous volcanic eruption. In those apocalyptic flames, Durdasa turned into an amorphous pile of ashes within no time and collapsed on Duryodhana's body.

Yudhisthira shouted; "What did you do you foxy and guileful Srikrishna? Durdasa was most loyal to me."

Srikrishna told in a contorted voice "Keep quiet you moron. If Durdasa did not burn into ashes in the flames of Gandhari's eyes, how would you be coroneted tomorrow as Hastinapura's king? This is politics... Such sacrifices of these loyal and allegiant Durdasas in the blazing furnace of politics is a routine thing. You should not be so aghast by such a small and negligible incident, Yudhisthira."

Sanjaya told in an abject voice, as if struck by a lightening: "What did you do great lady? You destroyed in your own hand the last insignia of the Kaurava race, Durdasa."

Srikrishna feigned compassion and said: "Mother! Who says you are sonless? Who are the Kauravas and who are the Pandavas? They are all your sons. Now accept the Pandavas as your sons."

Another mysterious smile floated on his face.

Gandhari looked down at the mango-bud-like fallen body of Durdasa at her feet and laughed boisterously in a frenzied manner and said: "I have understood everything Srikrishna! I have understood your foxy manoeuvres. But mark my words you congenital crook. You can never retain the throne by dint of your Sudarshan wheel's power. Everything shall be burnt by a grieving mother's curses. Even you won't be spared Srikrishna. Like the Somabansa, the Yadubansa[7] shall one day perish through internecine conflicts. Even your favourite son Pradyumna won't be spared. This is my curse, the curse of a mother who has lost her one hundred sons in the battlefield. My curse won't go in vain. Remember that Srikrishna. Remember that."

Crying inconsolably, Gandhari collapsed on the ashes of Durdasa.

There was another mysterious smile on Srikrishna's face which however was engulfed by the approaching darkness.

In the marooned sky above the Indraprastha mountain range, the blazing sun was also preparing to set in the west.

---

[7]   Lord Srikrishna's clan.

The Soul of the Dinosaur

I

The train ran hurriedly over Rupa Bridge.

Maharaja[1] Rai Brajeswara Rai lifted the shutter's glass screen, condescendingly, and looked outside, carelessly, through the window. In the eastern sky, a reddish streak of light was coming out slowly, like an ornate bride emerging from her chamber and walking slovenly towards the marriage pedestal. The morning approached like a blushful lady slowly lifting her enshrouding veil of darkness.

Brajeswara Rai's head seemed heavier due to last night's overdose of whisky.

Yes... Rupa Bridge. Below the bridge, River Rupa's zigzag stream lied on the sand like an exhausted woman who had slept with her partner last night. Who was this sensuous and concupiscent woman? Madhavi? Mohini? Srimati? Anuradha?

Brajeswara lighted the extinguished cigar. Nothing really had changed in the last ten years. The same recognizable landscape on the very familiar banks of River Rupa! The same old station of Rajkanchangarh right in front! Nothing had really changed.

A span of ten years was nothing. Brajeswara took off his woollen sleeping gown and threw it sloppily on the bed.

Returning to Rajkanchangarh on this wintry morning even after a gap of ten years made his drunken head fresh and

---

[1] King

rejuvenated. The train slowed down while whistling deafeningly during its final approach towards the old, dilapidated station-yard. From the platform a loud chorus of multiple voices rose; it was in fact a glory-slogan sung by the congregated public in the Maharaja's honour. Brajeswara listened with keen ears... "Victory to Maharaja Brajeswara Rai... Long live Maharaja Brajeswara Rai." His cruel and savage iron-face got slightly wrinkled with a thin ray of sepia-tainted smile that flickered only for a few countable moments, and vanished into the moist air like a tiny, little bird.

The train stopped inside the station-yard for a few minutes. Brajeswara peeped through its window and looked nonchalantly at the platform. After an enforced exodus for ten long years, he had today returned to Rajkanchangarh, with the lost grandeur of a dethroned king. The platform was heavily crowded to welcome him and no single space lied vacant and unoccupied inside its dreary and sepulchral premise. Of course, a lot had changed in these years. Rajkanchangarh had no more remained a kingdom; the kingship was gone and along with it was also gone royalty and its ostentatious grandeur.

The proliferating rust of growing age on Brajeswara's iron body was eminently visible...

He opened the door of the compartment with a condescending expression of disdain on his face.

Three servants quietly came inside. One of them quickly dressed him in his conventional regal attire; another held a water pot and a towel to him so that he would wash his face and then wipe it; another one brought the morning tea in a tray. Outside the compartment, the public went on chanting relentlessly 'Long Live Brajeswara Rai'; it went on repeatedly like the collective chanting of some divine mantra. His belongings were unloaded from another compartment. Lots of guns, many boxes, cameras etc.! Brajeswara slowly descended from the train's coupe onto the platform. It looked as if the tranquil morning sky trembled in the public's glory-slogan. Brajeswara's face was almost invisible from within the piles of dew-laden, marigold garlands.

He smoked form his pipe and asked someone: "How are you Mahapatra? Are these all Rajkanchangarh's people?"

Nilambara Mahapatra answered: "These are Rajkanchangarh's people, Your Excellency. Listening to the news of your arrival, they have accumulated here since dawn; these are the ones who have bedecked the gates with gorgeous designs and have placed festooned pots on the roadside for your grand welcome.

******

Another ten-year-old memory floated before Brajeswara's eyes like a momentary flash of an extended vision. It was the tale of a dark and sombre night in September, 1942. The British political agent Mitchell Sahib told him in a whiskey-drunken, drowsy voice: "Brajeswara Rai! You have to leave Rajkanchangarh right now by the orders of the mighty British government. It's an exile of ten years for you."

Outside the Rajkanchangarh palace, the agitated mob stood lined with country-made rifles and dynamites in their hands; they wanted nothing else but the tyrant Brajeswara's blood. This Nilambara Mahapatra had that day clandestinely led Brajeswara to safety and had left him in the railway station. He was the most trusted lieutenant of this cruel and ruthless king. After Brajeswara's compulsive exile, Nilambara also spent three long years in prison for being the former's notorious accomplice in many of his atrocities on the public.

Mahapatra shouted at the mob: "Give way you rascals. Give way to the king."

A Roles Royse car arrived within moments and parked outside the gate with great difficulty. The accumulated mob was pushed away by Mahapatra and a few of his accomplices with virulence and disdain. Brajeswara promptly got into the car without glancing at the gathered people. Nilambara Mahapatra quickly climbed onto the driver's seat and started driving the vehicle.

Though Brajeswara's appearance had undergone multiple transformations over the years, the same regal cruelty persisted on his scraggy, emaciated body. The same bestiality sparkled on his pale, lacklustre forehead filled with clusters of dishevelled hair. His age-old heinousness glittered through the penetrative vision of his razor-sharp eyes.

Brajeswara told: "Drive fast Mahapatra! I should reach the fort in an hour and fifteen minutes." The fort was seventy miles away from the railway station; but the vehicle ran at a speed of only ten miles per hour due to the blockade caused by the assembled public.

Mahapatra increased the vehicle's speed a little and told: "Sir! It's really difficult to drive fast through the mob."

They would have just met with an accident. A person was hysterically rushing in, to garland the speeding vehicle's bonnet.

Brajeswara shouted at the mob: "Fools! Morons! Don't you know that obstructing the public road is a punishable offence?" Then he instructed Mahapatra to drive even faster.

But Mahapatra argued; "Sir! These rascals have come from long distances to honour you, Your Excellency."

Brajeswara left out a mouthful of smoke into the air through the car's open window and said: "One day this ignominious bunch of rascals came from long distances and accumulated here to drink my blood. Neither their love nor their enmity has value for me anymore. I cannot act before them with folded hands. You drive fast, Mahapatra. You drive fast."

The vehicle vanished with loud horns in the midst of a raising whirlwind of reddish dust.

II

In the sprawling garden of the Rajkanchangarh palace, Brajeswara loitered with a barrel-gun in his slender, scraggy hand.

In the blue sky flew innumerable flocks of cranes, kites and sparrows filling its empty space with their loud and congregated twitters. Somewhere else, across the sky flew another flock of teal-ducks, like a garland of jasmines gliding aimlessly on its long-stretching, bluish floor. Brajeswara aimed at them and fired from his gun; some of the birds fell on the ground being hit by his bullets. A feeling of extreme contentment bloomed on his stupendously glazing iron-face. A gardener ran to search for the dead and the injured birds.

Another flock of birds came flying with loud twitters in the sky.

Their thirst for life was not quenched at the Caspian Sea. Its chilling winter propelled them towards the equatorial areas for the life-giving warmth that the latter offered. On their wings there was the mysterious allure of distances; in their throats, there was the mellifluous song of life. . . Brajeswara aimed at them once again and fired from his barrel gun. Some till ducks dipped through the air fluttering their wounded wings and then, fell on the ground. From their kaleidoscopic wings dripped tiny, delicate drops of blood onto the soil whose crispy sand was drenched in red.

Brajeswara lifted one bird in his hand in condescending cruelty. Death was slowly engulfing the bird like a baneful spell of sorcery cast on it by an invisible and devilish sorcerer. Brajeswara threw the bird on the ground without the slightest feeling of remorse or mercy. Of course, it was another matter that these days he no more enjoyed such rampant wastage of energy in gunning down birds. There was no excitement in these heartless killings anymore. He slovenly strolled back towards the palace placing the rusted barrel gun on his shoulder.

The soporific white shade of the palace danced on the adjacent pond's crystal-clear water like an adroit classical dancer. Brajeswara was startled by the restless twitter of a bird from within a tranquil cypress bush. The palace looked still, quiet and tranquilized, bereft of anybody's pulsating presence around. An atrocious and meaningless futility reigned over the whole ambience that had turned uncharacteristically sterile and comatose. Everywhere there was the empty profusion lifelessness. Brajeswara leisurely walked towards the palace with a downcast head.

In the front portico, some people were waiting fortuitously to greet him. At the news of his arrival at Rajkanchangarh after so many years, large contingents of citizens from his lost kingdom flew from distances every day to meet their king. The kingdom was lost; the kingship was gone; yet, their love, loyalty and allegiance for the dethroned king still lingered in their subconscious—firm and unshaken like a sacramental bond. Looking at Brajeswara, they paid him obeisance by prostrating before him. Brajeswara did not pay any heed. He took off his gun from his shoulder, handed it over to a servant and quietly went inside the palace.

Inside, he asked Mahapatra: "Why has this senseless bunch of people assembled here? What do they need? Drive them away."

Mahapatra said: "Your Excellency! The way time is changing, it's both beneficial and profitable to keep them in hand. Shall it be appropriate to drive these rascals away when they have come from distances with so much of love and adoration for you?"

Brajeswara answered in a slightly agitated voice: "Yes! Times have changed. But I have not. Neither do I have any desire to change."

Mahapatra left.

Everywhere there was the cruel, pitiless laughter of atrocious destiny! And also the meaningless profusion of regal opulence... The multicoloured rose garden was clearly visible through the open window. It seemed to Brajeswara as if his life was nothing but an attractive lady's beautiful and polished marble statue. She could be felt, but could not be enjoyed; she could be drunk; but that won't quench his thirst. Inside the shining and colourful ambience of the palace, Brajeswara felt terribly alone, distraught and incapacitated. His violent and irrepressible desire for flesh burnt into flames inside his desiccated veins and then was extinguished in a moment.

Brajeswara called: "Who is there?"

A servant rushed in and stood before him with a downcast head and waited for an order. Brajeswara ordered: "Whisky and Soda."

They were brought immediately. He sipped some whiskey from the glass and placed it on the nearby table.

Mahapatra came in and told: "Your Excellency! Damodar Raiguru has come to meet you".

Brajeswara asked: "Which Damodar Raiguru?"

Mahapatra told: "The same Damodar Raiguru of Ranidaha

who had girdled the palace with armed rebels in the blinding depths of the night during the citizens' revolt. Let me send him back by bluntly telling him that you cannot meet him."

Brajeswara said: "No! Send him straight to me, Mahapatra. Send him straight to me."

After some time came Damodar Raiguru, a fairly aged man with slackened skin and sunken eyes. The hair on his head flew like cornstalk in the wind. He had been a participant in many revolutions against the British government and had been imprisoned many a times. The grievous torture that he received in jail was still visible on his face as a clear and inerasable imprint. Damodar paid regards to Brajeswara with a bow.

Brajeswara asked: "What new demands do you have Raiguru? I have fulfilled all your demands."

Raiguru smiled gently and said: "What demand, Your Excellency? Nothing! Things are going from bad to worse here, in Rajkanchangarh."

Brajeswara told: "That is quite ok. You are destined either for the good or for the bad. God almighty has written nothing more on your forehead."

Raiguru asked: "Means?"

Brajeswara lighted his pipe with a characteristic display of heedlessness and said: "The meaning is very simple Raiguru. To exploit is the nature of man. He created the nation to protect the weak from exploitation by the strong. But the nation became more atrocious and exploitative than the man himself. Tell me who had thought of it?"

Raiguru asked: "Then why did we put an end to monarchy?"

Brajeswara left a mouthful of smoke from his pipe and answered: "There was a huge flaw in monarchy, Raiguru. I was exploiting and torturing the citizens without their consent; but democracy does the same with their consent. For instance, in monarchy, I could crack your head without taking your permission; but in democracy, I can do the same with your kind permission." After uttering these words, Brajeswara started laughing loudly.

Raiguru said: "Even I have started believing in exploitation, Your Excellency. Man does not rely on anything else other than exploitation. The human civilization, society, culture, and religion—everything is built on the foundation of fear. As long as there is exploitation, the human society shall continue to remain safe and secure. If there is no fear of exploitation, then man cannot be bonded in the incarcerations of the society."

Brajeswara left into his room. He did not want to further engage in such futile discussions.

III

It was evening.

Brajeswara stood near his rest room's window and looked at the moon-blanched garden sprawling outside like a colourful carpet spread out on a ragged and pebbly landscape. From within the thick foliage of the Eucalyptus and casuarinas trees, the full-blown moon rose slowly like the hallucinatory image of an unknown prince in the dreamy eyes of a despondent princess. Brajeswara had finished off all the whiskey from his glass in one, gigantic gulp. Coming back from the window, he sat languidly on a decorated sofa while looking vacuously at a kaleidoscopic chandelier that dangled from the roof like a gaudy fragment of memory. It dangled like a piece of reminiscence from his old, lecherous and despotic days. The severed heads of some hunted down tigers hanged on his wall as taxidermy. A hunger brimmed on their huge, ravenous tongues that looked awfully detestable and terrifying. The ageless hunger for flesh persisted on them even after the tigers' death while a ghostlike silence reigned over the dingy room's murky atmosphere. Inside, the dim electric bulb emitted clusters of unrecognizable, thin rays.

Brajeswara pressed the electric switch of the calling-bell. Within some time, Nilambara Mahapatra came in with hastened steps. Brajeswara lighted his pipe and said: "The evening looks beautiful and sensuous, Mahapatra."

Mahapatra said: "Yes, Your Excellency! It looks really beautiful."

Brajeswara left a mouthful of smoke from his pipe and

told: "But Mahapatra! The beauty is not to be enjoyed alone. Have you arranged for something? I mean a delicate, fleshy virgin— untouched, uninitiated..."

Mahapatra answered with the tone of an apologist: "Sir, gone are those days when we could drag anybody to your feet with force or money. The time has grown difficult."

Brajeswara said: "What is the problem? First there was the fear of the ruler. We could confiscate anything from anybody by the sheer display of power and might. Can we not do the same now?

Mahapatra answered with a clear and unambiguous gesture of disapproval: "I don't believe so, Your Excellency. It cannot be done now."

Brajeswara took another peg of whiskey and drank it silently. Then he lifted the emptied glass before his eyes for a few seconds and told while surveying something mysterious inside it: "I have heard Mahapatra, you have a rare piece of diamond inside your own house. Why should you look for it outside?"

Nilambara Mahapatra's eyes lit up like two burning pieces of coal inside a mine. His expressions became harder, complicated and unexpectedly rebellious. He said in an enraged and unapologetic voice: "I am indebted to you for life, Your Excellency. But I have not eaten up my conscience. No father in this world can accept such a dirty and detestable proposal. I cannot believe that you can be so outrageously savage and unabashed."

Mahapatra prepared to leave while thumping his feet violently on the ground. Brajeswara called form behind: "Listen Mahapatra."

Mahapatra stopped like a statue in a slavish response to Brajeswara's inviolable orders. Brajeswara kept loitering with a few silent steps inside the room and told: "You have violated your conscience many a times in the past to maintain your deathless allegiance to me, Mahapatra. And you know that quite well. Don't you remember how many hundreds of times you have compelled hapless fathers to send their daughters to me?"

Mahapatra said with folded hands and in a softened voice:

"Forgive me, Your Excellency. I cannot do it anymore. It's my own daughter."

Brajeswara threw a bunch of keys at Mahapatra and said: "Open that iron safe."

Nilambara Mahapatra obliged like a robot. It was full of sparkling gold jewelleries. His eyes lit up at their blinding resplendence.

Brajeswara said: "The royal mother had preserved them all for the royalty's future queen. You know Mahapatra! I love to confiscate things rather than obtaining them as gifts or by soliciting them like a beggar. And nobody knows it better than you. But rest assured that no single lady has worn these ornaments even once. If you wish, your beautiful daughter can wear them."

Mahapatra kept staring at Brajeswara unblinkingly like a hypnotized man. Brajeswara told: "I shall decorate her in my own hands as per her wishes."

Mahapatra sat on a couch like a dumb and immovable stone-effigy.

Brajeswara told: "I am waiting. Send her quickly."

IV

The night had deepened into an immense and inexplicable quietude.

Outside, the full-moon-night's moon descended down the horizon like a lost, celestial traveller. The palace-garden slowly got enshrouded by a thick cover of darkness.

Brajeswara poured the last few pegs of whiskey into the glass and told: "Sundari! You have a beautiful name. There is no exaggeration in it; it's easy and simple and truly justifies your elegant, fine-spun and supple body's unmatchable delicacy and splendour. You are truly beautiful, Sundari. You are truly beautiful."

Sundari was Nilambara Mahapatra's daughter. Brajeswara had heard it right. She was incomparably attractive and sensuous.

She stood near Brajeswara with a downcast head that was

half-buried in her breasts. She trembled like an injured deer hit by a hunter's arrow. She did not have the courage to look at the lecherous Brajeswara's ruthless, drunken face.

Breaking the silence, Brajeswara told: "Why don't you come closer, Sundari? Why do you stand there alone?"

Sundari didn't say anything and stood mum with her head buried in her breasts.

Brajeswara advanced towards her and lifted her veil while holding her exquisite chin in his right hand. He could readily spot a dark mole.

Brajeswara told in a seductive tone: "Sundari! This mole looks gorgeous and provocative like a bride's secret desire."

Sundari kept quiet like a dumb cow.

Brajeswara undressed her in both his hands. She stood naked before him, like the shy, bashful moonlit night bereft of the cover of darkness. Her pliant breasts were thoroughly uncovered. Her thick, delicate thighs looked like being carved in polished marble by an adroit artisan by sheer diligence.

Brajeswara told: "It's a beautiful symmetry, Sundari. It's a beautiful symmetry."

Sundari blushed and covered her face with her hands.

Brajeswara removed the remaining dresses from her body.

While resisting, Sundari's hand inadvertently hit the dark mole on her chin. The mole got partly erased and ran haphazardly along her softened cheek like a shady, unclear line. She had in fact drawn it in collyrium to make her face look more appealing, winsome and seductive.

Brajeswara said: "Your mole is erased now, Sundari. What was the need for you to paint your rosy cheek with a brush?"

Thoroughly denuded, Sundari sat on the sofa with her face covered by her hands. She had mixed feelings of shame, fear and apprehensions. She looked like a charming stone-carved effigy sculpted by an adroit artisan.

Brajeswara kept loitering silently inside his room with his arms folded against his chest. The thudding sound of his shoes engulfed Sundari's faint and almost inaudible heartbeat like a ravenous beast.

Finally, he stopped near her and asked: "Can you tell Sundari which is more beautiful? The moonlit night or the enticing nudity of your body?

Sundari kept looking at him dumbfounded, speechless.

Brajeswara opened the iron safe in his own hands and said: "These are all yours, Sundari. You take whatever you like. Your price! I am leaving. You can bolt the door from inside."

Brajeswara left the room and started walking through the night without direction. Undressed, Sundari kept watching him dissolve in the moonlight like a faint and unrecognizable shadow. Brajeswara kept walking and walking across time's endless trajectories, into the dark and circuitous depths of History. He was turning into a gigantic animal, a quadruped with huge, protruding canines, and sharpened claws and a prolonging, thorny tail. He kept sliding into the depths of the night and into the dark, dungeon of cruel time. He was a dinosaur.

The Capital City

The alarm bell rang like someone's shout: "Get up! It's seven in the morning..." Another day resumed. Subodh was always afraid of the day's beginning as it was going to be horribly taxing, without any doubt. He stopped the clock's lever bearing an overt expression of irritation on his petulant, swollen face. He wished it rang after fifteen minutes.

The morning light had not yet reached the room tearing the thick, velvety veil of the night. Everything was a conglomerate mixture of shades, of liquid darkness and faintly glimmering light; Subodh stayed immersed, for the time being, in this little, kaleidoscopic fiesta of colours. On the table, the flower vase looked like a cluster of crumpled dreams. Subodh did not feel like sleeping anymore. He pressed the calling bell on the table for bed tea and the morning newspaper.

These two addictions were his morning needs. He required tea to reactivate his incapacitated and hibernating nerves. And he required the morning newspaper to involve in a clumsy mess of nonsense: whether our nation is able to produce aluminium as per its requirement or not, what the president of the United States of America told in the banquet-meeting, how many children are dying in Congo every day due to malnutrition, how fresh our prime minister looked yesterday morning, what are the chances of war with our neighbouring countries etc. These might have been questions relating to his professional life; but for him, these were futile and meaningless things in life. "Your profession burdens your life; but your life does not control your profession.

This formula between your life and your profession is the real tragedy." Subodh told himself and continued: "I wish I looked into the matters of my kith and kin rather than looking into those in my surroundings. Today's newspaper is all about the life and the activities of industrialists, underworld dons, a few self-styled monks, cricket players and film superstars. These news items do not encompass the pains, pleasures and vagaries of life. There is intoxication in them."

But this was Subodh's profession... He was a special correspondent of a famous daily newspaper of the capital city.

Most of his time was spent in press conferences, in five-star hotels in the midst of freely offered lunches, coffees and dinners by various government as well as private agencies and organizations. And in between all these, he kept typing his report in his typewriter, willy-nilly, with a stoic and abysmal indifference.

But Subodh jovially called these invitations meal-tickets and termed these conferences free lunch sessions; his funny nomenclatures, of course, were imbued with clandestine notes of humour and sarcasm. Fascinatingly, however, there was a lot of competition amongst his friends and colleagues for these meal tickets.

Recently, there was a mammoth congregation of a few national leaders in the capital city. Amongst them, someone was a democratically elected leader; someone was a dictator and someone was a ruler whose rule might have ended anytime, through a military coup and another group might usurp power. The media reporters danced to their strange, bizarre and inexplicable tunes and projected them as national leaders of tremendous global relevance and significance.

These so-called global, national leaders were all cordially invited to the capital city to establish peace and harmony in the world. It was believed that even though they did not possess money, arms and ammunitions; they certainly had a collective voice that could create an impeccable, cosmopolitan impact.

Subodh was in no way interested in this congregation and thought that it was better to see a cricket match on TV rather than listening to these national leaders and applauding their dresses, their cuisine, their style etc. on the close circuit TVs in the media centre.

The editor however was a little annoyed with Subodh's characteristic and quintessential nihilism and told: "It's a mammoth and career-changing assignment, Subodh. There is a lot of hue and cry over it, amongst the public, and the ever-wakeful intelligentsia. How can you be so cynical and reluctant about an event of such magnitude, of such global significance and grandeur? I am surprised."

Subodh answered: "There is no novelty and innovation in these assignments, Sir. And thus, they don't attract me, at all. As simple as that!"

"What do you mean?" Said the editor, leaving a mouthful of curly smoke into the air from his pipe. "This will be one of our biggest achievements as hosts."

Subodh answered back: "Sir! This country has seen so many farces like this. This is another one. Nothing new in this!"

The editor said in an irritated gesture: "You are an incorrigible cynic, Subodh! You always see the opposite and pessimistic side of things."

Of course, this allegation on Subodh on the editor's part was not entirely unfounded. If he could accept everything with an easy-going contentedness, he would have attained peace and happiness in life. But his life was full of a flurry of adversities, hardships and complications right from the beginning; nothing came to him with ease and effortlessness. He had seen life's ugly face from close quarters and his bitter experiences had snowballed into a strange and bizarre mental derangement, an incurable psychosis. He had presumably inherited it from his forefathers. A sinful attitude indeed!

Subodh further told the editor: "Sir! My cynicism has always helped you to comprehend things better, to estimate things more correctly."

But for his quintessential cynicism, he had become a repulsive and loathsome alien in his journalist community. One relished being safe and protected inside a congregation and there was pain and suffering in aloofness, in standing alone on the top of a mountain and looking vacantly into the silence of the valley with the sombre and dismal eye of a cynic. But Subodh perhaps relished being alone.

Finally, this global conference came to an end. Subodh's reporting was widely acclaimed and extensively admired, not only across the journalistic brotherhood, but also from various quarters of the intelligentsia who particularly relished perusing through Subodh's reported news items. Even a press-attaché from the embassy's palace had profusely congratulated Subodh on his unique and efficient reporting.

Subodh had taken complete leave for one week after the conference. Today was the last day of his leave.

He took a few sips from the cup and stroked, absentmindedly, his long and curly strips of hair with his own hand; he did it to break his sleep.

An engagement pad lied open near the bed-lamp close to the teapoy.

This capital was the city of multiple events—a symposium on poverty to be inaugurated by a minister at 11 am in the convention hall of the five-star hotel Vikramaditya, a dinner party in the moonlight club, the birth day party of Santa Saxsena etc. A man without proper dresses and etiquettes had no place here. But Subodh only knew how hollow and picayune from the core was this elegant, flashy and catchpenny elite culture? But still one had to succumb to such sophisticated requirements of high society and to gleefully entertain its grandiloquent and magnanimous show of falsity, its glittery, falsifying facade. Otherwise, what was the requirement for him sending an ornate and glitzy flower bouquet along with birthday wishes to Santa Saxena? Subodh promptly dialled a telephone number in Hotel *Blue Diamond*, ordered for a staggeringly spectacular bouquet of orchids and roses and sent it to Santa Saxena's room. Then he spoke to her and wished her a very very happy birthday. Subodh imagined, sensuously, that she was holding the bouquet in her hands and caressing the orchid and rose-clusters against her cheek and saying in a sleepy and languid voice: "How lovely! How lovely!"

The paralysed Mr. Saxena looked at Santa while squatting—

helpless and incapacitated—on his wheel chair and told: "The bouquet looks fabulous. Only a lovely lady like you should own it." And then there was a little, incandescent flicker of a smile on his face.

Mrs. Saxena kissed her husband on his forehead and said: "O! How naughty you are!"

But was there an arresting, sensuous ecstasy in that kiss? A heartfelt intimacy in that embrace? Was there an unquenched thirst of ages in those apparently amorous moments of togetherness? Clearly, now it was not possible between them primarily because of their huge age-gap and also for Mr. Saxena's paralysed body's irretrievable decrepitude. Santa, though approaching forty, still looked young, dashing and refreshing. Mr. Saxena had once published an advertisement in the newspaper for a companion because he had become alone and depressed after his wife's premature death. Santa had carefully studied all the information regarding how much of share Mr. Saxena held in big companies, how huge was his bank balance, and how many palatial mansions he owned in different metropolitan cities. The companionship ended in marriage.

That day Santa had come out her palatial mansion in a certain pretext and Subodh had by chance confronted her inside a coffee house.

Subodh asked her in a carefully crafted, sentimental tone: "Santa! Are you really happy with this marriage, with this seemingly mismatching conjugal life?"

Santa took out a cigarette from her vanity bag, lighted it and said while smoking the cigar: "Nobody is perfectly happy in this world under any circumstance, Subodh. It is only money and profitability that matters, and matters most. That is the unscripted law of our sublunary existence. Mental peace and happiness are only futile, irrelevant, old-age words."

Subodh did not enquire further, being fully aware of the discomfiting sensitivity of the matter. Santa's previous husband had divorced her. She also had legion, miscellaneous material needs and expectations. Mr. Saxena was also leading a very lonely and deserted life.

But why did Subodh need to poke his head into Santa's private matters, unwarrantedly? A lot of women like her had entered into his life like multi-coloured rainbows and had gone out like perennially shifting, vacillating clouds in the sky.

Santa would also go like them.

The telephone rang. Someone asked in an authoritative voice: "Is it Subodh Kapoor speaking?"

There was a spotted a frown of irritation on his face, surging like a gigantic hillock of wave in a convalescing sea. Again, this boring character! The voice on phone said: "Hello Subodh! This is Professor Dr. Malhotra speaking."

Subodh answered in a clandestinely irritated voice: "What's the news?"

Professor Dr. Malhotra! It was all a hoax. This Malhotra was a mere lecturer in a private college once. Now he calls himself Professor Dr. Malhotra. In this capital city, who cares for in which subject you have completed your Ph. D.? What was your thesis?

Malhotra was a huge hoax. But in today's politics riddled with tawdry show-business and nepotism, these hoaxes topped the list of successful people in the society.

Prof. Dr. Malhotra said: "Subodh! We sat together once a few days back. Let's sit today again. I have a nice thing for you."

Subodh did understand what was the meaning of a nice thing? A nice thing meant sophisticated foreign liquor. Dr. Malhotra was the union president of the fourth-class employees of the foreign embassy. Through them, he could arrange such 'nice things' quite conveniently, that too without any cost.

But the real danger that lied in accepting his invitation was that at the end of the drink he would prod you to send a report on something to the newspaper and then, publish it. A fabricated eulogy on the foreign minister, for instance! And then he would say: "The foreign minister is visiting the United Sates this weekend. This statement should be highlighted in the newspaper before his departure." And after finishing off four pegs of whiskey offered by him for free, one could hardly refute his request. Like a letterhead company, Professor Malhotra was a celebrated leader possessing the prowess to influence even the fourth wall of democracy—the media. Sometimes he could even send you in a foreign visit either in a friendship-association or in some high-level delegation. He was either the president or the secretary of half-a-dozen friendship-associations.

But Professor Malhotra and a few more like him never understood how meanly and condescendingly the foreign diplomats of the embassy looked down on them for their cheap and sleazy priggishness for free scotch and whiskey. They thought that these people could be easily bought and sold for a few bottles of whiskey; for them, these were no more than ignominious herds of purchasable and sellable commodities. And they could shamelessly lobby for their own interests through these conveniently merchandisable people. Theses sycophants were flooded everywhere... from the embassy to the parliament.

Sycophancy and nepotism were the fundamental principles of the capital city's politics. The bigger a sycophant you were, the more successful a politician you could be.

Professor Malhotra asked on the telephone: "Why do you keep quiet Subodh?"

"We will sit together another day, professor. There is an urgent engagement this evening." Said Subodh and kept the receiver down in a snappy and cantankerous manner.

After the end of today's symposium, there was still ample time left in the hand. Subodh told himself: "I can go a little late to Santa's dinner party tonight and spend that time sipping whiskey in Professor Malhotra's house. But he was also overawed by the latter's agonizingly oily and casuistic behaviour, that at times looked awkward and terribly inconvenient.

Pretension and deception were the ingrained, mental features of the city politicians. They pretended about the greatness of their leadership qualities in the newspapers. That was their satisfaction.

This Professor Malhotra was an unabashed creature, to put it straight. To give attendance in the embassy was his everyday business, though it was not always possible for him to move inside and meet the diplomat. But once upon a time he had some sort of closeness with him. The latter once told him, perhaps out of a friendly goodwill-gesture, that he can go a long way in life. Capitalising on that, Professor Malhotra declared outside, overwhelmed by a mirthful and dreamy exuberance, that he is an important person of the embassy. He also declared in his friend-circle that the honourable diplomat intends to make him the corporator of a big city. The news also reached the other sycophants surrounding the diplomat for some personal benefits and for their long-cherished dreams to be fulfilled. They got envious and tried very tactfully to instigate him against the professor. On one occasion when Professor Malhotra was coming out of the palace after presenting a flower bouquet to the diplomat, one of the latter's acolytes told him point blank on his face, in a very clear and unambiguous voice: "Mr. Professor! People in the palace are not particularly liking your regular and unsolicited entry into the embassy. It's better if you come less frequently to the palace." Professor Malhotra immediately understood the gesture behind such words and gradually, his entry into the embassy was getting restricted. And it did not take him long to understand that the real diktat was indeed from the diplomat himself, in a clandestine and surreptitiously implicative manner though, for he never told things directly to anybody on his face. He always passed the information to the targeted person through his acolytes. Even Prof. Malhotra was also doing this job in the past. So, he could understand the implications even better.

These days, he stands beneath a mango tree inside the palace and welcomes the visitors with benign, folded hands. While he welcomes them, one could readily spot on his face the serene and assuaged smile of Lord Buddha and while greeting the people, he lifts his right hand in a benevolent posture, as if to bless his devotees like the Lord himself. Amongst the visitors are usually the rich people, businessmen and industrialists from different places and everybody who comes inside the embassy knows Prof. Malhotra, in some way or other. And Professor Malhotra tells them: "You please go inside and meet the diplomat. I am always at your service."

Self-aggrandisement in the media is an essential survival-tactic for people like Professor Malhotra. But for that, of course, they have to arrange a lot of good things (branded liquor) for the journalists. But of course, it is not a big thing for the president of the fourth-class employees of the embassy to smuggle a few branded liquor bottles outside the embassy. Professor Malhotra was adept in this business. Even his biggest enemies would accept it, unequivocally.

But it was also becoming increasingly irritating for Subodh to publish Professor Malhotra's statements in the newspaper for a few pegs of whiskey, a chancellor cigarette-packet and a cheaply offered dinner. But Professor Malhotra was in no mood to leave Subodh. He telephoned him again: "Subodh! If you do not come, the evening will be spoiled." Subodh answered with clenched teeth and with a succinct expression of cantankerousness on his face: "Sorry! Thanks."

No! He also did not want to go to Devinder Singh's breakfast anymore. This Devinder Singh is also another notoriously cunning character in the capital city. He is a sub-agent in a European military aircraft manufacturing company. A lobby is always required for selling aircrafts and for a lobby, one requires clandestine, negative advertisement against other competing aircraft manufacturing companies. And for this, one needs the cooperation of many — starting from parliament members to the journalists. And that is why it was a regular thing for Subodh to get invited to breakfasts, lunches or dinners into Devinder Singh's Jorbag palace. But slowly he had started disliking this business of sycophancy. He telephoned Devinder Singh and gently apologized for not being able to attend his breakfast invitation.

Then he got busy preparing for a symposium on poverty in Hotel Vikramaditya.

If his vehicle's carburettor did not trouble him, Subodh could have reached the symposium in time. But when he entered the hall after checking in at the reception counter, only a few minutes of the esteemed leader's speech had passed. The audience applauded his talk with passionate and vigorous clappings. Perhaps the great leader had delivered an extremely valuable harangue.

After the leader's speech was over, a costly safari-suit-clad gentleman climbed onto the stage, eliciting a phrenic and highbrowed demeanour. He stood on the stage in a dramatic posture, threw back a few braids of hairs from his forehead and started defining poverty: "If poverty is not correctly defined right at the outset, then all endeavours for its removal would be tantamount to swimming through condensed fog. All these ardent brainstormings would go in vain if the very word 'poverty' is not correctly defined. A high-level committee must be constituted to first define poverty, correctly." Then the gentleman went on...

A huge and rambunctious round of applause from the audience filled the thin air of the hall; the gentleman mistook it as an emotional response from the audience as an appreciation of his talk. Even the esteemed leader greeted him with a benevolent smile. However, the gentleman failed to understand that the audience's clapping was a purely a customary thing, a mere reflex action. They clapped for every talker.

The second speaker looked like a congenital rebel—Professor Roshan Lal. A very well-known face in the leftist, intellectual circle! He was a faculty of Sociology in a very reputed educational institution dominated by leftist orientations. He wore a thick 'khaddar' trouser and Punjabi and a pair of thick-framed, zero-power spectacles on his eyes. From his shoulders, hung a 'khaddar-cloth-made' Santi-Niketan-bag. A beard on his chin along with a few deepening frowns ravaging across his forehead attributed to him the precious and sophisticated look of an intellectual. Professor Lal took out his thesis from his bag and again kept it inside and then, started his speech in a slow and calculated voice which however turned fiery and vigorous within moments like blazing lava emanating from a volcano: "Whatever the previous speaker said is nothing but the repetitions of the voices of the capitalists, of the multinational company owners." The essence of Professor Lal's speech was that unless these exploitative capitalists were removed from this nation, poverty alleviation could never be achieved; it would rather go on increasing. Another uproarious round of applause filled the hall's exited and intellectualized air.

Now it was ten minutes to one o' clock.

Everybody was busy with lunch.

It was 3 o' clock and the lunch was over—a lunch that had five courses of different items.

In the afternoon session, came to speak Professor Lakdiwala—noted Gandhian economist. He was also outrageously opposed to the nation's capitalists, but for a different reason though. In his opinion, the only route to poverty-alleviation was the adoption of village-economy and promotion of small-scale industries. For him, the nation required no power plants. Cow-dung-gas would suffice. As long as there was 'charkha[1],' what was the need of a textile plant? Gandhiji of course had gone up to a single stitching machine. Not more than that! Of course, looking at the vastness of the nation, one might need trains and aeroplanes. But why would one need these sophisticated things in a competition-less village economy?

Professor Lakdiwala, keeping in tune with his communist ideology, wore a pair of motor-tyre-made shoes, a 'khaddar' dhoti that ran feverishly up to his knees, a half-shirt, a long beard below his chin and a pair of thick-framed looking glasses on his eyes. He was completely bald-headed, but never hesitated to speak and act in exaggerated and melodramatic manners whenever necessary. He spoke his mind without any inhibition. He started his speech:

"Poverty is nothing but a 'thinking.' It has nothing to do with economy. You won't find a village in our country from where a guest will come back in empty stomach. Families, who cannot afford to eat meal twice a day, will also arrange a meal for the guest. Such mental richness makes them survive in the midst of this circumambient, cataclysm of poverty. So, poverty can never be alleviated without inculcating in the public's mind a profound sense of mental richness. Otherwise they will remain both poverty-stricken and mentally impoverished."

Prof. Lakdiwala went on and on...

But perhaps his speech did not touch anybody's sentiment.

---

[1] An indigenous, wooden tool to weave clothes. It was used by the father of the nation Mahatma Gandhi to do the same.

After his speech got over, of course, one or two people gave a few customary claps, willy-nilly. But it was also an indication of the fact that many people, who did not clap, did not agree to his ideas.

The participants looked at their watches in worried and fidgety gestures. After devouring heavy, sumptuous meals, they did not have the patience to listen to another boring speech on poverty.

Subodh also did not have that patience. He came out of the discussion hall. For him, it was all sheer wastage of time and a fake, concocted show of intellectuality.

He typed the report in the newspaper room in the evening. In his report, he duly highlighted the ingenuous statements of Professor Lakdiwala; but his writing was in fact an acute and fierce criticism of such fake, phony and counterfeit facades going on in the nation in the name of intellectualizing poverty. However, the news editor put huge red and blue cross-marks on his writing and admonished him: "Mr. Subodh! If you continue to write like this, acerbically, then you will be very soon fired by your boss. So be careful in future."

Subodh answered: "He is most welcome to do that, Sir."

Outside, the evening had grown dense and pithy. Steeped in gas-light, the roads looked colourful and different. Subodh did not feel like going back to his flat; he dressed himself up for Santa Acharya's birthday party. Before driving to Santa's place, he parked his car outside a garden and went inside to sleep flat on its grassy lawn and to kill the day's boredom by looking vacuously at the starry night sky. He ran his fingers through his greyish hair and told himself: "Even this will do."

At least there was no faking in the evening's slow, intoxicating wind and in the night's caliginous darkness.

While driving his car into the golden premises of No. 3 Moonlight Colony, Subodh felt had he not reached in a wrong address? No-This was No. 3 Moonlight Colony. He was well-acquainted with that place. To clear his doubts, he stopped his vehicle in the midway and looked at the roadside Eucalyptus trees. No! He had not made any mistake. Today was Santa Saxena's birthday party. Below the portico was parked her imported Limousine car and no other vehicle or human 'being' was visible inside that huge, sepulchral premise. The big compound and the duplex looked morbidly empty and mournfully sombre. The bright halogens outside the glass windows and doors had exacerbated the tranquillity of the surrounding.

"But where has everybody gone?" Subodh asked himself.

While coming out of his car in a disturbed, lackadaisical manner, he met a uniform-wearing servant on the veranda. The servant saluted him.

Subodh asked: "What is the matter? Why others have not arrived yet?"

The servant answered: "The invitation was at 8.30, Sir."

Subodh looked at his wrist watch and was surprised to find that it had stopped at 8.30. Something had gone wrong with it.

He was a little dejected and despondent that he had missed the party. To relieve his mental agony and tension, the servant told him in a softened voice: "Sir, please go to the drawing room inside. Sir (Santa's husband) is resting there."

There was no use going back. Subodh went inside. The drawing room looked piteously empty and enervated. Another servant was cleaning the sofa and the centrepieces with a broom. Another one was busy embellishing the flower vases with different-shaped flowers. Subodh, of course, was not at all an unfamiliar figure in this place. The servants greeted him with salutes and requested him to sit comfortably inside the room.

But Subodh was very restless. He asked: "Where is madam?"

He knew he could meet Santa another day in some gathering in a party somewhere. But if he meets her today alone on the occasions of her birthday in this tranquil, captivating moment, he would definitely take her by a pleasant surprise. There was excitement in giving her such surprises.

Someone said: "Madam is inside her bedroom."

Today Subodh wanted to give a surprise to Santa as if it would have been the most precious gift for her on her birthday.

He walked stealthily, like a clandestine leopard, on the carpeted stairs towards Santa's bedroom on the upper storey.

Santa had not bolted the door from inside. The light inside the room was sparsely visible through the thin fissures between the door and the door screen. Subodh's flagrant eyes lit up with naughtiness. He thought Santa would be ecstatic to see him alone near her after such a long time. He lifted the curtain slightly from outside and peeped inside the room.

Santa sat languidly on a small mahogany chair in front of her glitzy and sumptuous dressing mirror. She looked lost inside herself, narcissistically. Seemingly enamoured by her own reflected image in the mirror, she had perhaps forgotten the situational immediacy of her environment. She looked frozen to stillness just like the frigid and fragrant cosmetic bottles and boxes, languorously placed on the dressing table. It looked as if she was acquiescently hypnotized by her own image on the mirror.

Before taking a new make-up, Santa had gotten herself rid of all the previous make-ups. Beneath the new make-up, nevertheless, lay concealed the many vermiculate wrinkles on her face, the many abrasive scars of her growing age, the many grotesque frowns beneath her two sunken eyes and finally, the growing, repellent, ugliness of her dwindling youth.

It was a horribly putrid and sickening revelation for Subodh to see Santa without make-up. Her bob-cut hair was the envy of many women; it was an object of attraction and adoration for her male friends like Subodh; it was the insignia of her glowing youth and beauty. But O God! What was this? It was a dull, pestilential wig. Subodh could not believe his eyes. The wig lay abandoned on the gaudy and shimmering dressing table like a dead thing.

Santa had already become bald-headed. The baldness of her head glimmered unsavourily   in the dimly ocular efflux of pinkish, rubicund electric light in the room. Some scattered locks of her clammy, caliginous hair hanged dishevelled from her head. She looked like a ghost, a gruesome apparition of an ugly and obscene silhouette in the dark. Even her curvy eyebrows looked fake and feverishly artificial. She had decorated them with her hands.

Subodh stealthily walked down the stairs. It looked as if he had no strength in his feet, neither did he have the old excitement to join Santa's birthday party.

It seemed to him as if Santa Saxena was the true insignia of the capital city's pretensions.

Vagabond

I

Athorough gentleman! He has a handsome monthly earning and has a decent family life with his wife and son. His bank balance has increased of late; but along with it has also increased his body fat. And along with them have also come dyspepsia, diabetes and blood pressure. This family life has given him pleasure. Oh!... While shaving, his blade slipped off. Kamal started bleeding. Oh! This growing age gives nothing but pain; it gives you death every moment. Kamal bled from his chin.

He took out his handkerchief to wipe off the blood. The silken handkerchief emitted the fragrance of 'evening-in-Paris' perfume. Mallika told she will come today. Kamal, half-shaved, got up, went to the door and locked it from outside. He lifted the half-broken railing of the window and came back into the room, and washed his face with soap. Then he emitted a long, deep sigh of relief. It was a beautiful idea. He could always lock the room from outside and sleep inside, peacefully. By doing so, he could fully avoid the nagging and cantankerous house-owner, the noisy and vociferous mixture-seller, and of course, Mallika; they would think that Kamal is absent as the room is locked from outside. Kamal lifted the half-broken window's rusty, fuliginous railings and came into the room, and washed his face
with soap. Then he emitted a long, deep sigh of relief. It was a wonderful idea; he could always lock the room from outside and sleep in his room, peacefully.

*****

Kamal travelled back in time through the memory lane.

That day Mallika was sleeping on his chest in the secluded corner of a park. Kamal said: "Mallika! I don't believe in love. A man does not have emotions; he does not have sentiments; he does not have soft feelings. He believes only in one basic, primitive instinct—lustfulness. Love is his incarceration; marriage is a confinement. But woman needs love. For that, she needs a man. That's why she loves her man and loves him more than her life. But for a man love is nothing but unconditional surrender. And I hate surrender, Mallika. I hate surrender."

Mallika said; "You are a cruel man, Kamal! You are a cruel man. You know Kamal! How much I have suffered by falling in love with you? Can you imagine what terrible pain and agony I have undergone in getting enmeshed with an unemotional, vagabond like you?"

Mallika's gown was full of the 'bloomed-lotus' embroidery.
She was a sub-inspector in the Police Department. She was chubby, dusky-complexioned, big-toothed.

*****

Nine o' clock in the morning! On a plane sheet of paper, Kamal scribbled the whole day's routine—willy-nilly, absentmindedly. He had to catch hold of that rascal Basant first.

Kamal took out a cigarette from the ash tray and lighted it.

He met Basant and they engaged in a coquettish, friendly conversation. Kamal said; "Basant! You are not only stupid, you are a big moron. Hey idiot! You were giving singing-tuition to some students and were earning something, and that was your earning for the whole month. Now you have left that. Then how would you manage your expenses?"

Basant said: "O! That is true. I had not yet thought of it. But Kamal! If there is no vigour of life here, then how can there be music? Why are these girls learning music? Sometimes I feel like getting asphyxiated before these girls. Ok... Can you lend me twenty rupees? The house owner is a monster. He has confiscated my harmonium. Now he eyes on my table."

Basant threw his long hair towards the back of his head.

*****

It has been six months since then. There was no news of Mr. Basant. Gone were also those twenty rupees.

Kamal said to himself: "Today I have to catch hold of the other fellow, Sripati Babu. Sripati Chaudhury! Lake Road! What is today's date? Monday! In which nostril I am breathing right now? Left nostril! Breathing in the left nostril on Monday! It's a positive premonition. Hey Mother Kali! Hey Mother Shyama! I wish Sripati Chaudhury does a life insurance policy with me today. I heard he is ready for an insurance policy of one lakh rupees. I will enjoy its commission for the whole year. Oh God! This coat has lost its iron and has become wrinkled. But it's still manageable. But where is Mallika? The ugly Mallika? Ugly both in body and mind! But what is the harm in marrying her? It does not matter even if she has a hundred affairs. Still she has a body that can be enjoyed. Her body is good enough."

It was already eleven. No! There was no news of Mallika. Kamal wiped off his face with a handkerchief. The fragrance of the 'evening-in-Paris' perfume was right in his nostrils.

II

Oh shit! Kamal hit a boulder. His boot-sole cracked at the right corner. This rascal road-corporation! The whole road is full of boulders and potholes. Nobody bothers if half of your foot goes. You will get some iodine and some cotton from the nearby dispensary and your injury will slowly heal. But at least eight rupees will be required to repair this cracked sole. It's actually the cost of a cigarette packet. It also means ten tension-free dreamy moments. Or else, four cups of special tea!

The next street is the fish-market-street. Then there is the Broadway Restaurant.
Below the coat, there was a monstrous beast gnawing the inner walls of his stomach with its sharpened nails. Hunger!

Kamal said to himself: "I need a cup of tea. Yes! Only one cup of tea! My nerves have become dormant. One cup of tea is five rupees. One pack of cigarette is ten rupees. The bus fare is twenty rupees. But I have only ten rupees in my pocket. It's better to walk to Sripati Chaudhury's on foot."

Kamal started walking.

III

A big road! Some cobbler was calling: "Shoe-polish Sir! Shoe polish! Don't you need shoe-polish, Sir? Don't you need it? Your sole is cracked sir. Your sole is cracked. Your right finger is visible through the crack, Sir."

Kamal kept on walking heedlessly. After a few steps there will be the fish market.

He reached the number 3 fish market. But where was Mr. Basant Das? The door was locked. On a bench at a distance was squatting the pea-seller Mr. Khan while sipping tea from a cup, intermittently. "Perhaps he is also waiting for Basant. Oh God! I won't be able to meet this bloody fugitive Basant. The rascal has escaped." Kamal said to himself.

"Then I must meet Sripati Chaudhury. But again, his house is four miles away." Thought Kamal.

"Oh! Here comes Basant's house owner. He can give me some information about him." Kamal said to himself.

Basant's house owner greeted Kamal with a ceremonious hello and said: "Good evening Kamal Babu. Look at this Basant Babu. A thorough gentlemen! But see! He has not paid my house rent for months together."

Kamal answered: "Where is Basant Babu? I am also searching for him."

The house owner answered: "He has absconded. I have confiscated his harmonium from him. Now he has vanished after throwing his table in a corner of my house. He told me he is getting married and he will clear all my rents after marriage."

"Basant's marriage? When is he getting married? That day Mallika was also telling about a marriage." Kamal asked himself with a clear note of surprise.

*****

That day Mallika told Kamal: "Kamal! We will build our dream-home away from the clattery and dismaying din and bustle of the city. You and me, a small house, a greenery-filled hill at the back and a swiftly streaming river in the front, smiling at us all the time!" On another evening also, Mallika came to Kamal with the same marriage proposal, with the same boring, monotonous dream-talk.

Kamal told her with an intention to hurt: "Mallika! How many dream-homes have you constructed with other men before me?"

Mallika kept mum while smiling impishly turning her face away.

This Mallika is a strange creature. She can easily take any offence with a smiling face. She has forgotten her past; now she wants a family even at the cost of pain, humiliation and suffering.

That day Mallika's wig was decorated with beautiful red flowers. Red flowers on a black wig...

Mallika told while answering to Kamal's questions; "Kamal! Body and soul are two different things. I have looked for that soul in many bodies. But today, I have lost the beauty of this body at the age of thirty-five. What attraction will you find in this worn-out body of mine? But today I have come with the attraction of the soul."

There was the sweet and beautiful fragrance of the 'evening-in-Paris' perfume emanating from Mallika's scented body.

Kamal said: "Mallika! You and I are now far away from the din and bustle of the main town, in a tranquil bamboo-covered village. On all sides, there are sprawling green fields merging into the sky at the distant horizon. Let's enjoy the beauty of Nature." Mallika left after some time.

Kamal said to himself: "There is a peace in this surrender. There is no shame, no torture, no humiliation in self-protection. Basant has taken the right track. Nobody can escape from the society. There is no point fighting with the opposite sex for nothing. There is absolute peace and bliss in this resistance-less, surrender. This fight is meaningless. Om Shanti! Shanti! Shanti! This is wasteland... Above is the sprawling, blue firmament of the sky."

IV

A little distance away!

After taking a right turn from the Motiganj Street, there was the flashy and elegant 'Chaudhury Mansions.' Sripati Chaudhury's Mansions! The blessed son of destiny! He can make an insurance of at least one lakh rupees. Kamal offered him a cigarette. Mr. Chaudhury said: "No thanks!" While trying to persuade him for the insurance, Kamal said: "See Mr. Chaudhury! Great poet Bharati has said: "Nalini Dalagata Jalamati Taralang (Life is like a tiny water droplet on a lotus leaf)." Bharati? Or Magha? Or Bana? Or Kalidasa? Or Shankaracharya? Kamal could not recollect. But he continued; "You must have heard Mr. Chaudhury that in America, the girls insure even the moles on their cheeks. Even the hair on their heads!" Kamal's voice looked convincing and persuasive though Mr. Chaudhury did not look very convinced and left bidding Kamal a sharply stinging adieu.

Kamal left the Chaudhury mansions, put a cigarette in his mouth and lighted it to rejuvenate his gruelling body and mind. The prolonged dusk of the last spring! There were rows of Deodar[1] trees on both sides of Lake Road. It looked as if the whole world was sleeping. There was no street vendor, no 'shoe-polish-shouting' cobbler, no noise. Only, small piles of fallen Deodar leaves all along! Here there is no obstacle, no pothole.... Here, the motion of the universe is smooth and uncomplicated. A motor cycle raced past Kamal. The Deodar leaves flew into the air for a moment and then fell scattered on the ground like slain soldiers in a battlefield.

Kamal tried his luck another day. There was the huge 'Chaudhury Mansions' right in front. A Ghurkha[2] durwan[3] dozed near the gate like a tranquilized bear. Kamal stretched his coat with his hands to make it look ironed. The horn of a locomotive motor vehicle was heard from inside. The Ghurkha durwan got up from his sleep with a jerk and squeezed a bamboo stick beneath his shoulder, stood up and saluted to the man sitting inside the car and then, opened the iron-gate. A gigantic black-coloured car went out and raced into the distant horizon. Left behind were

---

[1]   A thin-sub-continental tree with long flowers.
[2]   A Nepali and Indian tribe.
[3]   Indian colloquial term for watchman.

clusters of spiralling smoke emitted from its silencer-pipe, small whirlpools of reddish dust from the road and a bunch of dry, desiccated Deodar leaves fallen from the trees.

"What do you want?" Asked the Ghurkha durwan to Kamal while squatting on his chair. The irritation was visible on his face for his sleep was disturbed.

Kamal told in a slow voice with clenched teeth: "I want your head." The durwan obviously did not hear it. While lighting a half-burnt 'bidi[4],' he said: "Sahib just went out. You cannot meet him today."

Kamal felt like smacking the durwan on his dilated nose.

V

Again a long, stretching road of five miles back! Kamal's legs were paining. He had to go back and give it another try the next day. There were only ten rupees left in his pocket. Of course, he had to come by bus the next day. The bus fare would be twenty rupees.

Someone threw a lot of ground-nut-chaffs on him from above. In the approaching darkness of the evening, Kamal looked at the man sitting on the wall nearby. Someone was happily chewing ground nuts sitting on that wall. Kamal felt like dragging that man's feet and then, throwing him on the ground. In the meanwhile, the man jumped onto the ground from the wall. In the dim street light, Kamal could see that he was no other than his friend Vinod, standing in front of him in a stylish posture with a packet of ground nuts in his hand.

Kamal asked: "What were you doing on that wall Vinod?"

Vinod answered in a taunting voice: "I was performing yoga."

Kamal asked: "What do you mean?"

Vinod said: "I mean yoga. I can see past, present and future, Kamal. I know you went to meet Sripati Chaudhury to make a life insurance for him. Right? But before you have just reached his house, he went on in his Packard car for an evening ride. Right?

---

4   A thin smoking pipe containing tobacco inside. It is smoked by many people who are addicted to tobacco smoke.

Kamal asked in a surprised tone: "How could you know this, man?

Vinod answered in a sympathetic voice: "Hey! I was watching it all from this wall. The moment you approached the gate of 'Chaudhury Mansions,' he went out in his car for an evening ride. I was watching it all from here. Then after getting a kick from the durwan, you are coming back with a downcast head. Isn't it right my friend? If you did not want a life insurance policy from him, then why would you have gone there? This is all sheer common sense my friend, sheer common sense. You do not need to be a rocket scientist to understand this."

Kamal asked: "But Vinod! What was the need for you to come so long from five miles away to sit on this wall and chew ground nuts?"

Vinod looked at him and smiled and then, both started walking together.

Vinod pushed the pack of ground nuts into Kamal's hand and said: "It's big, sad news bother. You know Mallika. She is a sub-inspector in the Police Department and gets a salary of two hundred rupees per month and also free lodging. A free, independent and healthy life she lives! I had proposed her to marry me. Let her be above thirty-five! Let her be ugly-looking..."

Kamal added: "Let her be thin-breasted, dark-complexioned, tall-toothed..."

Vinod said: "If I married her, all my problems would have been solved. I could have easily completed my research project on 'primitive human culture' without any financial difficulty."

Kamal asked: "But why would Mallika want to marry a 'good-for-nothing' creature like you?"

Vinod answered: "Hey idiot! This whole Earth runs on the principle of relativity. Everything is relative here. I may be a 'good-for-nothing' creature for you. But I am precious for Mallika. You know what she told me? She said: "Vinod! I have come with the beauty of my soul for you. My body has lost all its attraction at the age of thirty-five."

Kamal asked in an injured voice: "Then what? What did she say more?

Vinod said: "No! She said nothing more. I was till now hiding from her, from the ravenous appeal of her soul. But now when I have decided to marry her, I hear that she has already gotten married."

Kamal felt like falling from the sky and asked with an anxious voice: "Mallika has gotten married! When? To whom?"

Vinod answered: "I don't know when. But I know she has married that vagabond Basant Das. He was teaching her Sitar. That is when their romance started and then, he has married her. They have left the town yesterday somewhere for honeymoon."

Kamal said to himself: "Oh God! Everything is lost. My last hope for Mallika is also gone. With that also is gone the hope of getting back my twenty rupees from that rascal Basant. Now if I ask him that money, he will answer: "That money is our marriage-gift." Then also, Kamal had already looted a lot of money from Mallika in the name of being her ardent lover. But still, he thought this might be a golden opportunity for a making a life insurance policy for Basant. He thought he will go to him and tell: "See Basant! I am telling all this to you as your well-wisher. Now you are into family life. There are lots of responsibilities in family life, but there are also possibilities of untoward mishaps. So, to keep the destiny of your family secured, you must get a life insurance for yourself."

Kamal discovered another thorn in his sole. It was now impossible for him to walk any more with his shoes on. He lifted a piece of paper from the road, wrapped it around his shoes and kept walking with naked feet.

Vinod told Kamal: "Now do you understand friend? Why I was sitting on that wall and chewing ground-nuts, far away from the din and bustle of the city? I was doing so out of pure grief and frustration. I was cursing the universe for the torture that it has inflicted on me."

But Kamal could not so easily forgive that rascal Basant inside his mind. "Buffoon! He did not give me my twenty rupees. And again, he has also married Mallika secretly, without even informing any of us." Kamal said complainingly.

In the front, there was a restaurant.

One got very tasty prawn cutlets here. There was the

beautiful fragrance of prawn cutlet in the wind. Both the friends started smelling it. Kamal carefully scrambled for money in his pocket. The cruel beast of hunger had already started gnawing his belly from inside.

Vinod placed his hand on Kamal's shoulder and said; "Come friend! We are feeling very hungry."

Both of them got into the restaurant without wasting further time. First Vinod, then Kamal! Both sat near a table in the corner.

Vinod hit the table in his hand and called the restaurant-boy in a heavy voice: "Boy! Boy!"

Kamal said in a timid voice: "There is not a single rupee in my pocket, friend. There is not a single coin there."

Vinod said; "It's not easy to fool me Kamal! I have heard the jingling sound of coins in your pocket. Now you see what is in my pocket."

Vinod took out the inside cloth of his two pant pockets. Some ground nuts came out from them and fell on the ground.

Kamal cursed Vinod in a cramped voice with clenched teeth—shirker, idiot, dacoit, rascal.   In   the   name   of friendship, you called me to this restaurant and now you want to rob me off the last traces of my little treasure.

By that time, the half-pant wearing restaurant-boy had already come to the table and was waiting for the orders.

Kamal told in a helpless voice: "Four prawn cutlets."

A Hindi gazal[5] played inside the restaurant. Vinod started singing keeping in tune with the song.

The restaurant-boy came back with two prawn-cutlets in each plate and placed them on the table. Vinod put one cutlet into his mouth and started chewing it like a wild animal.

VI

The friends came out of the restaurant and lighted their respective cigarettes.

Kamal asked: "What next?"

---

[5]   A kind of Indian classical song.

Vinod answered while leaving a mouthful of smoke into the air: "The journey is aimless and also, endless, my friend."

Kamal remembered his dilapidated rented house in that dirty slum. The house-owner must be sitting on the veranda waiting for him for the rent and would be twisting his moustache to kill time. Once this image floated in his mind, all his courage to go back to the rented house vanished into the air like smoke.

Echoing Vinod's words, Kamal told: "Truly friend! The journey is aimless."

Vinod dragged one of Kamal's arms towards one street and said: "I am very tired, friend."

Kamal asked: "But where? You cannot enter the park at 12 o' clock in the night. The police will arrest us and we have finally to spend time in the police station."

Vinod answered: "No! It's not the park. It's the refugee camp in front."

VII

The refugee camp!

Initially, it was somebody's jute 'go down.' It was a huge asbestos-covered hall where forty families had taken shelter. It was also terribly hot inside. Therefore, forty small families were sleeping outside in the field, to get the cool, soothing breeze of the evening. Forty furnaces were burning out there. One furnace for one family! Somewhere boiled rice was getting separated from the boiling water; somewhere ladies were kneading breads. Along with that, there were the sounds of babies crying, the old folks shouting and the bangles of the ladies jingling intermittently. Vinod slept on a mat folding both his hands beneath his head. Kamal also placed the coat below his head carefully for the fear of its ironing getting destroyed. Oh! It was so peaceful. The calm, soothing evening breeze! Millions of smiling stars in the sky! And the stealthily approaching darkness! From a distance was audible the din and bustle of the city.

At some distance away, a lady was kneading the bread and then, warming it in the fire. Around her, her four siblings were looking at her like hungry puppies. In the light of that fire, her thin and scraggy face looked clearer. She looked like the living effigy of tolerance.

Vinod thought: "I have lost one relation. I need not be sad and broken. I will build another relation, another house. Man has survived through all bad lucks, all curses, and will continue to survive through them."

That lady took out one bread from the pot, made it into four parts and gave one to each of her four siblings, and then, put another bread on fire.

Vinod had started snoring.

VIII

Kamal has also slept.

You could call these people vagabonds. You could call them beggars. No issues...

Vinod had slept. But if he was awake, he would have gotten up and told: "I have researched into the whole of the human history from the old stone-age till today and found out that those who have not surrendered to the society and have remained aloof, have always suffered. Sadness, bad luck, humiliation and pain have been their eternal companions. But they have always searched for innovation and held to the society the light of newness. And in that light, the world has always rediscovered its identity. They may be the cursed human beings. The thin-breasted ugly Krishnas and Mallikas have come to their houses with the appeal of their souls. But these people have run away. You may call them lunatics, vagabonds."

But Vinod had always found evidence in support of these people from History.
Vinod had slept.

Kamal's snoring has become louder.

The lady has finished preparing her breads. Her four siblings had already slept.

The Gulmohar

The weekly newspaper *Sangram*'s office!

Sadananda looked at the proof. The age-old building stared at him like a grumpy-faced old man. The rain peeped in through the cracks of its concrete roof and went on splattering on its scorched face with its torrential deluge and profusion. Water streamed along the cracked floor, like tiny, miniscule, rivulets. On one side of the wall ran the blue cover of accumulative moss.

Outside, the August monsoon rain had subsided a little. In a feeling of exhaustion mixed with depression, Sadananda pushed the proof, irksomely, to the table's other corner. While correcting the proofs tirelessly, he had turned into a depressive cynic in the last few years. His life had been a compendium of mistakes right from the beginning till the end.

Four pages still remained for the finalization of the print—sixteen columns. They had to be meticulously edited. In a feeling of exhaustion and irritation, Sadananda brought out a piece of cigarette from his pocket and lighted it.

He was simultaneously the editor and the proof reader of that weekly. One more assistant was there to take care of the external things.

For some reason, Sadananda peeped through the office's ramshackle window and stared at the exterior environment. For the last many years, he could not even get a single, opportune moment to look outside and enjoy the natural vista with the keenness and passion of a romantic observer. He could not exactly count the number of days or months or years for which he had not looked at the external world so carefully.

A Gulmohar tree stood adjacent to the window. Beautiful—No! Only the word 'beautiful' would be an incomplete description of the tree. Its reddish blooms were gorgeous, soft, sweet and soothing.

In the August sky, the dark nimbus clouds weighed so heavily against the sky that it seemed as if they would collapse on ground, all on a sudden. And the lone Gulmohar tree looked like blooming in their lap like a gigantic, reddish flower.

The cigarette was finished. Sadananda threw it outside.

Sixteen columns more!

He closed the door violently. In a world made of docile and complaisant slaves, life for him had become no more than a futile, meaningless existence. He thought for a moment that he was living the life of acquiescent slavery in a world unceremoniously crammed with bustling swarms of slaves. Slavery has sucked the marrows form the bones of every free citizen of this world.

"Then what is the difference between a coolie form the suburb and Sadananda?" He thought. "The coolie is the slave of the mill-owner and the idealistic Sadananda is the slave of his own ideology. What is the difference?" He kept muttering to himself.

Even there is a sense of fulfilment in the coolie's life. The day he gets his salary at the weekend, he drinks to the lee with a sense of absolute contentment. But Sadananda did not have that luxury. A huge discontent brooded over his life right from the beginning till the end. And where was that feeling of contentment in his idealism? It was never there. Sadananda lived a life full of discontentment, of futile, lofty idealism and of unrealized dreams.

*****

The window opened on its own with a striking gush of wind.

The Gulmohar tree peeped at him through the window. There was a clear and perceivable sense of mockery and ridicule in its look.

Too many years had passed by now. One day he had decorated Tamasa's wig with Gulmohar in his own hands. It was a long time ago, when Tamasa came to his house as a bride. That was a lazy, intoxicating afternoon of a torrentially raining August.

Today, Sadananda's aging hands have lost their reflexes.

Sixteen columns more!

Sadananda came back and sat near the table. But how would he have finished these sixteen columns? The treachery of Britain? The growth of feudalism in Russia? The growing capitalism of America? Or the mental illness of India? Sadananda had lost his patience in writing such stuff again and again.

One could not however write the story of this Gulmohar tree in the newspaper. This tired, red Gulmohar tree—in whose reddish luxury, this silent, cloudy August afternoon had become uncannily fickle and mischievous.

No! This Gulmohar won't perhaps find a place in the editor's universe. The whole world would perhaps ridicule its description in a newspaper column.

The newspaper columns are meant only for politics where the act of living is nothing but a pretentious lie, where the greed for power, domination and exploitation awfully carries the only meaning of life. The Gulmohar has no place here.

Sadananda came back and sat near the tree.

But it seemed as if the tree had revolted against Subodh's cheap, narrow and constricted mentality. It had flown its grey banner of revolt throughout the world.

Sadananda got up from his chair like a man hypnotized by a sorcerer. Then he left the office and went outside.

The rain had stopped. Sadananda came back and stood below that Gulmohar tree. On the green grassland below were spread out innumerable, flashy and elegant red petals of its flowers carried away and scattered by the rain-splattered, stormy wind.

In Sadananda's every vein, there rose the fickleness of an early youth, like the recalcitrant waves of convalescing sea. He desired to climb up the tree and pluck the Gulmohar flowers as much as he liked.

But inside his own 'self' infested with proliferating infirmity traversing across his bones due to his growing age, he could not muster the courage to do so. If he climbed to the tree and plucked flowers at this age, then this unfeeling world would snub him, ridicule him. Sadananda carefully surveyed through at all directions with a circumspect and observant eye. There were human beings all around—innumerable, dirty, abominable bipods.

"Hey, Ramesh is coming here. He is definitely coming with some new complaint." Sadananda said to himself.

Ramesh approached him and told: "Sadananda! The press is closed. You are roaming here. Please tell me how shall the compositors get their salary by tomorrow?"

Sadananda shrugged nonchalantly and said: "I don't know.'

Ramesh asked in a stupefied voice: "What do you mean?"

Sadananda answered: "I really don't know. You go from here Ramesh. Please don't disturb me."

Ramesh came back from there, dumbfounded.

After some time, Sadananda also came back. Everywhere there were human beings, pullulating like mushrooms on a dampened surface. He could not muster the courage to climb up the tree and pluck the flowers.

Now it was late in the night.

In the cloud-infested sky, the pale and lumpish moon of the dark night had come out; it was showing its grumpy face with an iffy and sneaky disposition.

One ray of that gloomy moonlight had lavishly fallen on the sleeping Tamasha.

But there was no sleep in Sadananda's eyes. In these eyes was horridly dancing the reddish fickleness of the Gulmohar flowers.

Sadananda looked at Tamasha and said to himself: "This is the Tamasha on whose fragrant wig, one day I had embedded beaming and resplendent clusters of these flowers."

He muttered again: "No! This is not that bride Tamasha in whose effulgent wig, lay hidden the prehensile mystery of that night. That Tamasha is dead and gone."

Man dies. Man dies some day without his knowledge. The rest of his life, he lives the charmless and exiguous life of a slave.

Tamasha is dead and gone. Sadananda is dead and gone.

Sadananda left his bed and stealthily went outside to that same Gulmohar tree.

The tree was gleefully swaying the lambent, rubicund canopy of its flowers over the sleeping Earth.

Sadananda came and stood below the tree.

He tightened his dress to climb up the tree. But he felt as if he had become handicapped, limbless, incapacitated. He felt as if his whole body had drained itself off all its youthful energy, vigour and fickleness.

Still, Sadananda started climbing the tree, applying all his energy and strength.

Suddenly he heard a voice from behind: "Who is there?"

The constable of the night duty! He was clad with a raincoat from top to bottom. A stick in his hand! A half-burnt cigarette in his lips!

Sadananda got down from the tree.

The constable lighted his torch and focussed it on Sadananda.

"O you, Sir! So late in the night!" Said the constable.

Sadananda answered in an unprepared voice: "No! Nothing much!"

Before the constable spoke any further, Sadananda came back from that place with quickened steps.

He thought as if this Earth had died. Sadananda had died. The Gulmohar tree was only a tearful emblem of that once picturesque and vibrant life.

Night in the Metropolis

A steamer shouted desperately in the Ganga Jetty.
In the dim light of the light-post, Chaurangi's empty road looked like a mysterious and bodiless ghost from the underworld.

Chaurangi—the Mecca and Medina of business culture!

On the other side of the tram-road, clusters of refugees slept on the soil; below was the begrimed, dust-ridden land of the city, and above, floated, exotically, the tranquil night-sky like a dark, embroidered canopy. The roadside furnaces smouldered with fragments of burning coals.

The quiet moon walked unsteadily on the sky's stretched-out highway like a habitual drunkard. The dance party in a roadside western hotel was already broken and dispersed by now. From inside the hotel, few western-dressed men came out in every five to ten minutes and seeing them, the brokers waiting patiently on the Chaurangi pavement became alert and attentive. One of them asked me: "Salam Sahib! Salam! Do you want a girl?"

"Nonsense! How dare you say such a thing to me?" I asked the man in a heavy and irritated voice. But it was his business. The man was a little taken aback by my crude and discourteous response and then, said in a slightly apprehensive tone: "You do not have to go very far, sir; it's here, in the first bend of the Park Street."

I was surprised by the nagging and unscrupulous confidence of the man; he stuck to me like a shade despite my snobbish reprimand. Heedless of his unrelenting persuasion, I kept walking ahead while trembling all across my torso in a mixed feeling of shame and anger. I wished I could shoot that man as if shooting a dog. What a fallen, an abominable creature! But I was also aware of the fact that he represented a culture that reigns here, however crude and despicable it may be. I thought if one could be a respectable leader by brooking between the nation and the individual, if one could be a reputed lawyer by doing the same between the justice system and the client, if one could be a great sage by mediating between God and man, then why should a man be condemned for pimping between the flesh of an unfortunate girl and the bestial desire of a lecher? Strange are this pimp business and its culture, I thought. You never know one day this ignominious bunch of businessmen would end up selling this nation's soul. They would earn percentage for that—what's the harm?

Another one stood behind the pillar. Looking at me, he suddenly came in front and stood there, unmoved while casting surreptitious, oblique glances at me.

"Hey sir! Look at that advertisement board. It's not very far. It's there on the Park Street bend." He said.

I looked back. The first broker was getting inside a taxi with a western-dressed sahib. I did not pay much heed to that and kept walking ahead oblivious of what had happened so far. A horse-cab-man, while speeding up his boggy on the road, called in a loud-mouthed voice: "Come Sahib! Come! Bada Bazar! Bada Bazar! Park Street!" This was the third broker I met on the Park Street. I looked keenly at him. He went on narrating the place in minute details.

I asked him this time: "Is this your profession, your source of income"?

He answered quite confidently: "Yes sir! Percentage and tips give me good earning."

We approached the glistening advertisement board and then, trudged a little ahead.

*****

It was a beautiful, starlit night of March. The soil emitted volumes of heated vapour that seemed like intermittent warm sighs of Earth, surging into the nocturnal air with impeccable force and buoyancy. I felt asphyxiated. The roadside cotton trees were flooded with innumerable flowers; the skyscrapers looked like pigeon-nests from a distance containing thousands of families fallen asleep—husbands, wives, brothers, sisters, daughters... all of them.

I moved on. One street mysterious led to another sub-street which ended in a flat. Its upper storey was filled with clearly audible, rambunctious laughters from a few shameless, uninhibited drunkards. I knew straightway that I was right there in the middle of the much-talked-about Park Street end.

A man accosted me with a cacophonous voice from the upper storey by virulently hitting the bolt against the door. The door opened with an uproarious clang and a garishly attired lady appeared tantalizingly before me and I presumed that she was the flat's owner. I buried my disconcerted face down in shame, and was oblivious of my own thoughts and contemplations. The man pushed me a bit, persuasively, and told: "Sahib! Tips!" I readily extracted a five rupee note from my pocket and shoved it into that man's hand. He looked immensely happy and obliged and said: "Salam Sahib!" Then he looked ravenously at the Park Street lady and said: "Sister! Where is my due?"

I asked him: "What due?"

He said: "My percentage."

I pushed another five-rupee note into that man's hand and said: "Leave now."

That man went away whistling with a tone of extreme contentment. The Park Street lady looked at me with a visible sense of bewilderment and told: "Come in sir."

My mouth was drying up. I asked while getting inside: "May I have something to drink?"

The lady answered: "Sure sir!" She then called a girl by her name: "Minu! Minu!"

A small girl of thirteen or fourteen appeared on the scene with sleepy and apathetic eyes; her indolent face bore an expression of slight irritation and cantankerousness. But that lackadaisical expression, nevertheless, made her look even more charming and beautiful.

The Park Street lady ordered her: "Bring a glass of iced beer, Minu."

I was delightfully assured that the old lady has a gentility of taste. It made me happy. Minu left. Her sleepy and undulating wig camouflaged her back like the sturdy, caressing arms of an incorrigible lecher. A blood-red, fragrant rose was dredged deep into her chintzy and luxuriant wig. But the rose looked repugnantly pale and lacklustre.

I kept looking at her with transfixed eyes. The Park Street lady said: "Sahib! She is my sister. She has not been initiated yet. Till now, she is untouched, unblemished and uncorrupted."

She was sufficiently apprehensive from inside that I would straightway ask for Minu's flesh, unabashedly, like a profligate, incorrigible lecher. But has this flesh ever fulfilled the hunger of the body? This flesh is for the hunger of the mind. I could never have enjoyed this little girl; I could have loved her with parental affection.

Minu came back with an iced bear bottle on a tray and placed that before me.

The Park Street lady said: "Hey! Why didn't you bring cigarettes?"

Minu was going back to fetch cigarettes, willy-nilly. I interrupted and told: "I have cigarettes with me. You please sit here."

Minu sat beside me, reluctantly though. Her eyes were getting closed, perhaps due to impending exhaustion. I wished she could sleep on my lap and I could tell her the enchanting stories of the prince and the princess. The prince sitting on the will-horse, the princess on his lap, the will-horse flying away with the celerity of an arrow... And chasing them the gigantic monster from the cave...

Minu, while languidly flexing her body, told: "I am going, sister." And then, she left.

Her long wig cascaded her back. But she left me with a farrago of mixed but conflicting emotions—pity, sympathy, affection, hatred, love...

After Minu left, I looked at the Park Street lady again. She was almost forty with a slackened skin loosely cloaking her sickening body. Her growing age was emblematically visible through the proliferating wrinkles swarming across her progressively darkening face and bedimming eyes. However, she had tried her best to feign the appearance of a young and attractive lady. Her entire face was painted ruddily; she had laced rose-coloured lipstick on her lips; her cheeks had ruse splashed on them. But of course, all these cosmetics and extravagances could not minimize her age; rather they made her appear gruesomely ugly and unattractive; she looked ten years older. If she had a son, he would be my age.

I took clear cognizance of the damned place again. That flat of the Park Street bend... Two emptied beer bottles lay strewn below the Sofa... the ashtrays were nearby filled with broken cigarette pieces...

How terrible is this woman's figure? She is a daughter, a daughter-in-law, a mother
. . .; but today, her hunger has slaughtered them all with immense cruelty. She wants to live.

Her face reminded me of another woman.

That day I was travelling from Howrah in Delhi-Punjab mail. The inter-class compartment was heavily crowded and there was no space lying vacant for even a tiny, miniscule grain of mustard seed. I went standing from Howrah to Asansol. At the corner of a long berth, a lady sat on a blanket spread on the ground. Looking at me, she said: "How long would you go standing, son? Come and sit near me, here. Her kind and eleemosynary words overflew with motherly affection; her benevolent gesticulations were warmheartedly assuaging."

I sat near him shyly and noncommittally. But she made me comfortable by saying: "Why do you feel apprehensive, man? You are my son's age. He stays at Delhi. I am going to meet him."

Two half-circled, undulating, frowzy lines ran curvaceously from her nostrils to her cheek. But those lines did not look repugnant and unattractive; rather they looked soft, squashy and munificent. If she saw me somewhere on the streets, she would have called me 'son,' yearningly.

But today, it is the infamous and damned Park Street bend; it's fifteen minutes to two o' clock. The lady squatted before me with her artificial, pompous, ruse-powdered face that hid beneath its unfettered, flaccid skin legion anecdotes of pain, suffering, and misfortune.

The ugly and lacklustre evening's depressive monotony was growing unbearable for me. For a moment I thought it would have been better if I left this place.

I asked her: "What's your name?"

She answered in an inebriated, dreary gesticulation: "Chandra!" Then she told in an accustomed voice: "Please come inside, Sir! How long would you be sitting here?"

I extracted two ten-rupee notes from my pocket, instantly and pushed them into Chandra's jagged, asperous and pabulum hand and told: "It's already so late in the night. I am leaving."

Chandra was perhaps thinking that she has no justified right on this unexpected money. I could succinctly sense that and before she intended to say something, I banged the door open and said:

"Give half of it to Minu."

Chandra told: "But Sir! You have not even touched her." There was a strange and insalubrious sense of curiosity on her varnished face."

Her question hit me like a sharp arrow. The moon-burnt night of March suddenly turned poisonous and vexatious in that harrowingly ugly and discomfiting moment. One day, this childlike, innocent Minu would be touched, and initiated into this dirty, vulgar and pugnacious trade of flesh. Then the sleazy and shameless herds of luxurious lechers of the city would eat morsels of her flesh, one after another, like predatory, hungry wild beasts with their cuspidate, protruding canines; they would tear apart her body with their curvy, sharpened nails. And then the day when her flesh would be consumed thoroughly and their dirty desire would be fully consummated, she would be thrown away like a dry, desiccated piece of bone into the drain, for the ugly, scampering herds of street dogs, to devour and relish. A cold shiver ran through my spine like an electric wave, and a strange and unexplained agitation seized my nerves with impeccable force and virulence. But I had to control myself with restraint.

*****

It was twelve o' clock the next day. The same Chaurangi pavement, the same putrid, feculent question...

"Do you want a girl, Sahib?"

I slovenly walked along the Park Street bend towards that flat.

The same flat! The door closed from inside! I gave it a gentle push and it opened with a bizarre, cacophonous creak, inviting me eerily into its stuffed, turbid world of filth, of darkness, of unbridled savagery. Minu appeared before me with the lucent clarity of a reverie and said: "Come inside, Sir." I obliged like a complaisant and submissive adolescent and went inside, and sat on the Sofa exhaustedly dropping my haunch on its embroidered cushion. Minu's lotus-face looked decorously gorgeous and resplendent.

Then she told in a seemingly apologetic voice: "Sir! Two people are inside. My sister would just arrive. You please be seated. Let me go and bring iced beer for you."

But I told: "No! I want only water."

Within some time Minu came and placed a glass of water on the table and then, was almost leaving. I told: "Minu! Please sit here."

She sat on the corner with a mixed feeling of hesitation and apprehension."

I asked: "Where are you from Minu?"

Her two eyes abruptly turned schmaltzy and watery with my questions. Slowly two sparkling and recalcitrant drops of tear started rolling down her rubicund, cosmetic cheeks.

I asked: "Why are you crying, Minu?"

She told: "My home is far distant from here, Sir. We were escaping. My father was lost somewhere. My brother was hacked to death."

"My mother ended up being here..." Her voice was choking inside her throat; she was almost asphyxiating as if voluminous, warm vapours of grief and agony crammed inside the emptied spaces of her hollow and ravished 'being' were set to rise and rise with an explosive and convulsive outburst. I could understand that she had been sold in this street by her hapless mother who did so to alleviate her burden.

I felt like crying for the girl. But my blithesome tears had dried up.

I asked: Have you got some education, Minu?"

She answered: "Yes, I can read."

I took out a Rupakatha journal from my pocket and placed it in her hand and told her: "When you feel depressed, read this book."

With girlish swiftness, she rubbed her hand a few times on the book's kaleidoscopic cover on which there was painted the picturesque, eye-catching photo of an unknown prince flaunting his armoured chest with an exuberant display and gallantry and valour. He was riding the wish-horse, on a mission to free his incarcerated princess, from the clutches of a fiendish sorcerer inside an underwater castle.

Minu might be thinking the prince of her dreams would arrive. Or he might not come. The wings of the wish-horse might have broken inside a deep forest, at the bustling city's misty and foggy outskirts.

I could hear Chandra's approaching footsteps and that of her two drunken, brassy and reprobate customers form the stairs.

Minu left.

Those two customers also left. Chandra closed the door and sat beside me. She smelt malodorously of cheap, country-made liquor. I stepped back for the smell was repugnant, nauseating.

Chandra said: "Not here today, Sir. Let's go upstairs."

I was not at all willing to go upstairs, but could not resist my inquisitive temptations and followed her all along the stairs to the playhouse at the top. The whole inner space was daintily crammed with whisky and soda bottles and cigarette strays.

Chandra sat on the sofa. Her head was reeling with the liquor's acrid and dismaying hangover.

All on a sudden my eyes were fixed on a framed photograph

lying on her table. It was the photograph of a handsome, blazing young man. I stepped ahead to have a look.

Chandra flung herself onto me like a deleterious and cataclysmic storm and pushed the photograph inside the drawer.

I asked in a stupefied voice: "Don't worry Chandra. What is the harm in me having a look at your lover?"

Chandra burst into obstreperous gushes of tears, confiscated the photograph from my hand and lambasted at me in a throbbing, tearful voice: "Do you know Sir who is this man? He is my son. I gave birth to him after bearing him for ten months in my womb."

He was not a bastard child, Sir. He was the son of his father. They hacked him to death that day in front of my eyes. I have seen men turn into carnivorous beasts. They hacked my husband in a similar way. They spared me only for my body. I could manage to save myself with my body and come here.

Chandra hid her face in my chest and started crying like a baby. I felt like pushing her off due to the smell of liquor. But she was not leaving me as she might be feeling that crying like this might help her alleviate the prolonged, excruciating pain of her tormented soul.

After some time, she lifted her head from my chest and started wiping off her tears. They were washing off the paint from her face while exposing its darkish, mangled and diseased texture... ugly and horrifying. Her skin looked like the dark, ruffled and brambly surface of tin stripped off its tar. Two drops of tear were burning in her eyes, like two pieces of smouldering charcoals.

I hastily took out a fifty-rupee note from my pocket, pushed into her hand and said; "I am going Chandra."

Chandra told: "No Sir! I won't leave you, those two drunkards... those ugly, gruesome, beastly bastards... "

It was five minutes to two o' clock in the night.

I told: "No, I shall leave Chandra."

She grabbed me with her arms with impeccable force and virulence while pressing her lipstick-ridden lips against my face, violently, and told: "No, you can't leave Sir."

I felt as if someone was pressing a burning piece of coal

tightly against my face. With a sudden fit of anger and annoyance, I slapped her, inadvertently though, and told: "Leave me."

Chandra told in a stupefied and injured voice: "Sir.'

I told: "Not sir! If you would like to call me by some name, call me son. I would be your son's age if he was alive."

Chandra pressed her head against my face and cried: "O God!"

Outside, the cruel night reverberated tauntingly with that sound: "O God!"

Its echo was howling through the steamer's restless shout in Ganga Jetty.

www.ingramcontent.com/pod-product-compliance
Lightning Source LLC
Chambersburg PA
CBHW050142110726
47898CB00008B/2640